Under
SEAL

SEALs of Coronado

PAIGE TYLER

With special thanks to my extremely patient and understanding husband, without whose help and support I couldn't have pursued my dream job of becoming a writer. You're my sounding board, my idea man, my critique partner, and the absolute best research assistant any girl could ask for!

Thank you.

PROLOGUE

High Above the Pacific Ocean

HOW'D YOUR DATE GO WITH THAT GIRL I SET YOU UP with?"

Petty Officer Nash Cantrell opened his eyes to find his fellow SEAL—and resident ladies' man—Dalton Jennings, expectantly watching their teammate, dark-haired Wes Marshall, as they sat in the cargo section of the Air Force MC-130H Combat Talon II aircraft. Four years younger than Nash, Wes had been on the Team since the middle of last year, but as far as everyone was concerned, he was still the effing new guy—at least until someone newer showed up.

In the seat beside Nash, Wes shrugged. "Okay, I guess. Until it got weird."

"Define weird," Dalton said in his Southern drawl.

"Emily insisted we stop by her mother's

house so she could meet me, which was kind of different since it was our first date," Wes explained. "Then when Emily ran upstairs to grab something from her bedroom, her mom hit on me. She actually gave me her number and told me to call."

"Huh." Dalton shook his head. "Gotta admit, I didn't see that coming. What'd you do?"

Wes opened his mouth to answer, but Nash interrupted.

"Wait a minute. Back up." He looked at Dalton. "You set Wes up on a blind date?"

Dalton considered that way longer than he needed to. Either he did, or he didn't, right?

"I wouldn't really call it a blind date," Dalton finally said. "I mean, I showed Wes her profile on Tinder first."

Beside Dalton, the fourth SEAL on their four-man Team, Holden Lockwood, snorted but didn't say anything.

"I could set you up, too, if you want," Dalton told Nash. "There are a lot of women out there who aren't shy about admitting they want to hook up with a Navy SEAL."

Yeah, tell him something he didn't already know. Nash would have doubted the wisdom of letting a guy who had more women on speed dial than Nash had contacts in his phone setting him up with anyone, but after Wes got hit by a mother-daughter tag team, he was even more sure he shouldn't let Dalton play matchmaker.

"Thanks, but no thanks." Nash shifted in his seat. They weren't the most comfortable things in the world to sit on, especially if you were wearing all the gear you needed for a HALO jump. "I prefer to meet women the old-fashioned way."

Dalton arched a brow. "What, at the bingo games down at the VFW? Good idea, bro. Those gals definitely can't outrun you."

"Funny," Nash muttered.

Sometimes, he wondered why the hell he even bothered. He loved Dalton like a brother, but when it came to women, they might as well be from different planets.

Dalton shrugged, then rested his head back and closed his eyes. "Whatever. It's your loss. But don't ever say I didn't offer to help a brother out."

"I wouldn't dream of it."

Beside Nash, Holden glanced his way. The dim lighting of the plane's interior caught the angle of his slightly crooked nose, making the decade-old break look more pronounced than it really was.

"What do you have against Tinder?" Holden asked.

Some of the SEALs on the Team—like Dalton, and maybe Holden, too—had zero interest in getting serious with a woman. According to them, long-term relationships and being a SEAL were simply incompatible. Nash wasn't that cynical. Granted, he'd never gone out of his way to look for a serious relationship, but he also hadn't hidden from it either. Not that he expected it to happen anytime soon. After four failed relationships since joining the Navy, he wasn't holding his breath.

While some of the guys on SEAL Team 5—like his chief, Chasen Ward, and teammates, Logan Dunn and Trent Wagner—had lucked out recently and found women willing to put up with the crap that came with falling for a guy who risked his life on a daily basis, it was rare. In Nash's experience, a lot of women might be intrigued by the idea of dating a SEAL, but it wasn't until they started living the reality of endless deployments, training exercises, and late-night phone calls sending their significant other to dangerous places that they fully understood what it meant. Most bailed before they even got that far.

"Nothing," he finally said. "Checking some-one's profile out, then swiping left or right just isn't my deal. I'm more into the quality over quan-tity approach."

"Maybe if you're looking for a woman who can actually handle being with a SEAL long term," Dalton remarked, eyes still closed. "I'm interested in a woman looking to support the troops for an hour or two at a time. Why get involved with someone when she's only going to bail on you in the end?"

"Damn, you're cynical," Wes said. "Some woman must have really done a number on you."

The answer to that question was a definite yes, but Nash knew if Wes expected Dalton to fill him in on the details, he'd be waiting a long time. Nash opened his mouth to tell Wes as much when the klaxon alarm rang, announcing their ap-proach to the target. Nash automatically flipped down his night vision goggles, noting that his buddies did the same. The minute their personal oxygen was switched on, the jumpmaster lowered the back ramp of the plane.

Cold air rushed in, smacking Nash in the face as he fell in step behind Holden. Nash waited for Holden to step off into the pitch black night, then followed immediately after him. He knew Dalton and Wes would be right behind him. For a High Altitude Low Opening jump, it was necessary to stay in close formation as much as possible so they didn't get spread too far apart. Of course, that increased the possibility of them smacking into each other, especially with the way the swirling wind shoved them around. Things didn't get any better lower down, where rain started hitting them like a swarm of angry bees.

This was effing insane, Nash thought as he strained to find and then keep his eyes on the dim lights of the rapidly approaching container ship below him. Who the hell thought it would be a good idea to try to land a SEAL team on top of an ocean-going cargo ship in the middle of a torrential downpour?

Oh, yeah, now he remembered. It had been the CIA.

They'd thought it would be a piece of cake. But then, they weren't parachuting in with the team, which made things simpler. Life was always easier for the people sitting around an office with a cup of coffee in their hands, dreaming up impossible crap for the SEALs to do.

Even Nash had to admit that the ship—going

by the dull ass name of *MOL Deliberate*—had seemed plenty big enough when he, his team- mates, and the CIA analysts had gone over pho- tos during their three days of mission briefings. 1200-feet long, 160-feet wide, and loaded with a veritable parking lot of tractor trailer-sized steel cargo containers, it *had* seemed like parachuting onto the ship would be a piece of cake, even if it *was* moving at fourteen knots through the middle of the Pacific Ocean in crappy weather.

But now that he was dropping quickly toward the poorly lit ship as it plowed through rough, rain-shrouded seas in the middle of a pitch black night, Nash decided it wasn't going to be as easy as they'd thought. If the twenty mile an hour crosswind didn't make him miss the ship com- pletely and send him plummeting into the ocean, it would have the deck rearing up at the wrong time to break his legs when he hit. He wasn't sure which would be worse. One would be embarrass- ing while the other would be painful. Given a choice, he'd go for the broken legs. Bones healed, but embarrassment lasted forever.

On the other hand, he could always overshoot the bow of the *Deliberate* and promptly get run over by the quarter-mile long behemoth. It would be like getting keel-hauled by a pirate ship. Well, right up to the moment the big propellers chewed him up and spit him out. Yeah, he wasn't as crazy about that option.

When he, Dalton, Holden, and Wes finally left Syria after nearly getting killed in a missile attack on the Osprey they were in, instead of taking them home, their new transport had dumped them on an island in the middle of the Pacific, where they'd gone through three days of intensive training to get ready for this jump. That meant three days of listening to the CIA moan about how important this operation was, and how the SEALs had better not blow it. Holden had almost punched the lead training officer more than once. Nash had been more than ready to join him.

Nash pushed those frustrating thoughts aside and focused on working his steering and braking lines to get him on a glide path toward the barely visible masthead light near the forward section of the cargo ship. That aim point increased his chances of overshooting the designed landing zone and getting run over, but if he landed too far back, he risked someone on the bridge seeing him. That would kind of suck, too. Ships' crews tended to take a dim view of people parachuting onto their vessels in the middle of the night. Those merchant marine types had no sense of humor at all when it came to people they thought might be pirates. Probably had something to do with spending all their time cooped up in a big sardine can without cable TV.

The deck of the cargo ship—which was actually the top row of shipping containers—came at him fast. He tried to time his landing, hoping to touch down as the bow dropped through the backside of a wave. Unfortunately, it wasn't like he could sit around and wait for the perfect moment. Gravity was pretty much in charge. He was along for the ride.

Depth perception got a little funky the last twenty feet or so, even with the night vision goggles he wore. Nash yanked hard on his brake lines when he thought he was close, praying for the best. He actually flared out pretty well, losing most of his downward velocity, but then the ship came up to meet him when he hit, buckling his knees and knocking the air out of his lungs like he'd jumped out of a third story window. He instinctively dumped air out of his chute, but before he could get the thing collapsed, the crosswind kicked up and yanked him sideways hard enough to nearly tear his body in half.

He cursed as he slammed shoulder first into the metal top of the nearest cargo container. It wasn't necessarily painful, though getting slammed to the deck while carrying fifty pounds worth of gear wasn't anything to sneeze at. He only hoped his guys hadn't seen it. If they caught sight of him getting dragged across the top of the cargo containers like a plastic bag in a Walmart parking lot, he'd never hear the end of it.

Nash yanked as hard as he could on his chute, determined to ditch it even as he tumbled toward the side of the ship, hitting every sharp edge and projection as he went. What could possibly be worse than completely missing the ship and ending up in the drink? Landing on the ship and getting beat to crap as the wind dragged him around, then getting tossed into the drink anyway. That would definitely earn him a nickname he wouldn't want to live with.

He caught the edge of the last cargo container with his hand as he slid past. The move almost ripped his arm out of the joint, but it stopped him from going over the side of the ship. Sending up a prayer of thanks, he scrambled to his feet and quickly collected his chute. The plan was to be on and off the ship in ten minutes or less. The longer they stayed, the greater the risk of being seen, and this whole mission depended on no one ever knowing they'd been there. They were here to recon the situation, then disappear into the night, not to engage with any hostiles.

Balling up his chute, he tossed it and all his other unneeded gear over the side of the ship, ignoring the aches in his ribs, knees, and shoulders that suggested he was going to remember that landing come morning. Instead, he focused on moving as fast as he could across the heaving cargo containers, then headed toward the starboard side of the ship where he was supposed to meet up with the other guys.

Halfway there, he caught up with Dalton.

"I saw that landing of yours as I came in," Dalton said, throwing him a quick look as they ran. "I thought for a second you were dead, bro."

Nash grimaced, but kept moving. "For a second there, I thought so, too."

His friend gave him a quick scan up and down with his NVGs, no doubt checking for injuries. "You good?"

"Nothing a good massage and a bottle of tequila won't fix," Nash said.

Dalton grinned. "I can help you with the tequila, but you're on your own when it comes to finding someone to give you a massage."

Together, they dropped down from the top row of containers to the one below, then the one under that as they worked their way toward the main deck. If the CIA's intel was right, the particular shipping container they were looking for would be in this direction. Nash prayed the CIA knew what they were talking about. All these shipping units looked the same to him. If the stuff they were after wasn't where it was supposed to be, they'd never find it.

Nash poked his head around the next corner, checking to make sure the row between the containers was clear before darting across it. He and Dalton kept their voices low as they talked. Even so, Nash wasn't worried about anyone hearing. Between the rain, the wind, and the waves, he could barely hear himself think. Still, it didn't hurt to be careful.

Nash glanced at the dim lights of the bridge, using them to navigate his way through the maze of containers. They met up with Holden and Wes a few minutes later. The two were already picking the lock of a cargo container.

"Glad you guys finally decided to show up," Holden said without looking up at them. "I was worried you thought we'd landed on a cruise ship and were wandering around looking for the buffet on the lido deck."

Nash chuckled as Holden finished popping open the high-security lock. A moment later, he yanked open the double doors, then disappeared inside, Wes at his heels. Dalton quickly joined them, but Nash hung back to take a look around to make sure no one had seen them. Once he was sure they were alone, he followed the other guys into the tight confines of the cargo container and out of the pouring rain.

The inside was filled with stacks of metal boxes. While there weren't any markings on them, there was no mistaking that they were military ammunition containers. Holden took the lid off the one closest to him, then frowned.

"What's up?" Nash asked as he moved closer. "We are dealing with weapons, right?"

"We're dealing with weapons all right," Holden answered, never taking his eyes off whatever was inside the box. "But these babies are a little more serious than our friends at the CIA thought."

Curious, Nash looked over the rim of the box and cursed. They'd been briefed to expect your basic terrorists cache—automatic weapons, hand grenades, some bulk explosives, maybe even some rocket-propelled grenades. While all that stuff might very well be in some of the other boxes, that wasn't what had Holden so worried.

"That's a Russian 9K333 surface-to-air missile," Nash said softly, immediately recognizing the distinctive nose cover and the black thermal battery directly under the front of the advanced shoulder-fired weapon system. "This thing is as high-tech and deadly as it gets. Russia only gives these to their top-of-the-line troops and maybe a few of their most trusted allies. Nine times out of ten, this missile will take down any military aircraft, cruise missile, or unmanned drone in the world. Anything flying at low altitude at least."

"You mean like a commercial passenger aircraft on take-off and landing?" Wes asked.

"Exactly."

Shit. Missiles like this would be a terrorist's wet dream.

The CIA hadn't given them much in the way of details about the purpose of this mission, other than to tell them that the ship they were on was supposedly carrying an unspecified number of weapons to someplace in Mexico. Nash had assumed the stuff was destined for one of the drug cartels, or maybe a terrorist sleeper cell, but the CIA wouldn't confirm or deny where the shipment was heading or who was supposed to receive them.

Given the CIA's unwillingness to talk, Nash was surprised the Agency had come to them for help at all. Navy SEALs did a lot of crazy stuff, but slipping onto a foreign commercial ship in international waters to confirm the existence of illegal arms bound for Mexico had to be the wackiest. SEAL Team 5 and the CIA Special Operations Group had worked together on some crazy shit lately, but this mission was definitely out there.

Maybe the CIA knew the SEALs had the best chance of pulling off something like this. Then again, maybe the CIA preferred to have the DOD get the blame if this all went bad.

In the end though, none of that political crap mattered. People in pay grades well above them had decided the SEALs were going on this mission, so Nash and the other members of his team were here. But finding weapons like these suddenly made a simple mission drastically more complicated.

"I know we're only supposed to observe and report, but are we seriously considering leaving these missiles here?" Dalton asked.

It was a good question. The CIA told them to confirm the existence of the weapons, slip some tiny tracking devices into a few of the containers, then leave without a trace. In theory, the CIA would track the shipment to its destination then make their move. But would the CIA seriously be okay with allowing missiles like this get to a port in Mexico?

"Dalton's right," Nash said. "We can't let these missiles end up in the hands of terrorists or drug dealers. Even if we put GPS tracking devices in the cases, there's still a chance the CIA could screw up and lose them."

"I know, but no matter how we handle this, the CIA is going to shit bricks," Holden said, his eyes still fixed on the high-tech weapons.

Nash grunted. "They'll get over it. And if they have that much of a problem with how we decide to handle the situation, maybe they'll stop inviting us on these damn missions."

"Don't suppose we can just blow the things up, huh?" Dalton asked.

Nash knew that would be the easiest thing. A

couple blocks of C4 explosives and all their problems would be gone. That was the thing with explosives—they tended to solve a lot of problems. But explosives weren't an option on a commercial ship like this.

Holden realized that, too, because he shook his head. Slipping the lid back on the top container, he cinched down the latches, then looked at them. "No, we can't blow them, but we damn sure aren't leaving them here."

Nash's thoughts exactly. Unfortunately, getting off the ship with five containers full of missiles was going to be a lot more difficult than getting on it. Luckily, SEALs always made contingency plans.

He and his teammates moved quickly, putting tracking devices in several of the larger ammo containers they were leaving, then pulling the five missiles boxes out of the cargo container, and heading for the side of the ship with them. Once they had all of the weapons positioned alongside a clear section of the ship's railing, they sealed the missile boxes so they wouldn't leak then tied them together and attached flotation bags to them. Holden then hooked a tracking beacon to one of the boxes while Wes pulled the lanyard that would fire the gas generator on the float bags.

Nash stripped off his tactical gear, dumping most of it over the side of the ship until he was wearing nothing but the wet suit he had on under his clothes. A few feet away, his teammates did the same. The original plan had been to jump overboard, where they'd all float happily along until a Seawolf class sub lurking in the area came to the surface to pick them up. Their new plan involved doing exactly the same thing...while attached to five containers full of missiles. Explosive-filled missiles in the middle of rough seas. What could go wrong?

After the missile containers were in the water, Holden and Wes jumped in. Nash waited for Dalton to follow, but his buddy hesitated.

"If you don't make it through this alive, you can be sure I'll go out of my way to console all those women you don't want me to introduce you to. Just because I'm that kind of friend."

"Bite me," Nash said as Dalton hopped up on the low wall that ran around the perimeter of the ship.

"No thanks. You're not my type," Dalton said with a grin as he dropped out of sight.

Shaking his head, Nash leaped up on the wall, then stepped off into the darkness to join the rest of his Team in the frigid cold water.

CHAPTER
One

Mexico, Two Days Later

CRAP.

The moment Bristol Munoz heard her father coming down the hallway of the villa, she turned and quickly headed in the opposite direction. She didn't want to see him, much less talk to him. It wasn't simply that she hated him—though that was certainly enough reason all on its own. It was the fact that they couldn't be in the same room for five minutes without arguing. And she didn't feel like getting into a fight with him right now.

She glanced out the big picture windows at the jewel-like waters of the Pacific Ocean and beyond to the thriving Mexican port city of Manzanillo. The weather was sunny and beautiful, which meant it was a perfect day to wander around town—if she was ever allowed to go into town. She hadn't been outside the house that had become her prison in over a year. If her father continued to have his way—which he always did—she'd be stuck there for the foreseeable future.

She tried to walk as quietly as she could on the marble floors so she wouldn't give herself away as she headed for the library, but her leather flip-flops seemed to echo with every step. The library was her favorite room in the villa, with lots of comfy chairs and shelves upon shelves of books to lose herself in. It had been her mother's favorite room, too. That was one of the reasons Bristol liked it so much. The other was that her father never went in there.

But before she could make it to the double doors of her sanctuary, heavy footsteps approaching from the direction of the library froze her in place. No doubt it was some of her father's guards. There were never less than twenty of the heavily-armed goons wandering around the villa at all hours of the day and night.

Cursing under her breath, she ducked down a side hallway. Unfortunately, the only thing along it was her father's study, which was one place she didn't want to go. But she couldn't see an alternative, unless she went back the way she'd come.

Opening the door, she slipped inside, then closed it soundlessly behind her. She stood there a moment, leaning back against the wood and waiting for her pulse to slow. In the hand-painted portrait above the desk directly across from where she stood, her mother's crystal clear blue eyes smiled down at her. The painting was why this was Bristol's least favorite room in the villa. Not because she hated her mother. She loved her mother. No, she despised coming in here because it tore her heart out every time she saw the portrait. She couldn't believe her father had the arrogance to display a painting of the woman he'd so viciously murdered.

Bristol didn't realize she was still staring at the picture, tears running down her cheeks, until she heard the thud of leather-soled shoes right outside the door. Heart pounding at the thought of her father finding her there, she pushed the painful memory of her mother's death aside and darted across the room into the en suite bathroom just as the door to the study opened.

She held her breath as she heard her father

cross the room, sagging with relief when the expensive leather chair behind the desk creaked as he sat down.

"Is it wise having the weapons shipped directly to Manzanillo?" a man's deep voice asked. "Don't we have to worry about the other members of the cartel getting word of the deal?"

Bristol cringed. She wasn't surprised Leon Gonzalez was with her father. The big Colombian was her father's right-hand man and personal bodyguard. Luis Munoz never went anywhere without the creepy South American killer. You never knew when you might need to have someone's fingers cut off...or a bullet put in their head.

If possible, she hated Leon even more than she loathed her father because he was almost certainly the one who'd killed her mother. On her father's orders, of course.

Bristol leaned against the door, absently listening to her father and Leon talk about the pros and cons of shipping weapons into the local port, and whether there was a chance anyone else in the cartel would figure out what they were doing. As she eavesdropped, she replayed a recurring daydream she had, one involving the Mexican Federal Police smashing through the walls that surrounded the villa like it was a compound and arresting her father for being a murderer and a drug lord.

She wasn't delusional. Her father was a major player in the Amador Crime Cartel. The people who worked for him moved drugs, killed innocents, murdered cops, and anyone else who got in their way. It wasn't a leap to hope that someday the Federales, or maybe the Mexican Army, might show up to deal with him.

Luis Munoz had always been rich. As a little girl, Bristol remembered him taking her to the huge warehouses he ran down at the port. It wasn't until she'd gotten older that she'd learned he owned several shipping lines that moved freight all over the world. He'd acquired his first company—the one he'd owned when he'd met her mother—from his father, and had grown the business in leaps and bounds until he was the biggest freight hauler in this part of the world.

When she was twelve, Bristol had asked her father about all the armed men who guarded the villa and the perimeter walls that had begun going up shortly after that. He'd smiled and tickled her, making her laugh as he told her that he was an important man who needed guards and walls to keep her and her mother safe. His reasoning had made complete sense to her and she hadn't given it another thought.

That was the father she'd known when she'd gone to Connecticut to attend college in her mother's hometown. She'd come home Christmas and Spring Break, as well as in between semesters, but it wasn't until she'd returned for good after finishing her master's program that she finally picked up on the fact that something had changed.

The most obvious difference had been the increase in security at the villa and constant parade of scary people meeting with her father every night. Leon had shown up then, as well. But none of those oddities stood out as much as the tension between her parents.

Bristol's mother had come to Mexico after graduating from college looking to explore the world and meet amazing people. She'd met Luis Munoz her first night in Manzanillo and fallen in love at first sight. A day didn't go by when her mother and father didn't kiss or hold hands. When they didn't do either of those things after Bristol moved home, she knew something was different between them. She'd tried to talk to her mother about it, but her mom refused to say anything, other than to urge Bristol to go back to Connecticut to spend some time with her grandparents and get a job there.

Then Leon had cornered Bristol one night in the kitchen, invading her personal space and saying insane stuff about the two of them getting married soon. She'd still been trying to figure out what the hell he was talking about when the jerk had tried to kiss her.

In retrospect, Bristol probably should have shoved him away and gotten out of there, but she'd never been one to shy away from confrontation—something she'd gotten from her mother, she supposed. So instead, she'd slapped Leon. The bastard had hit her back so hard she thought she'd pass out. She hadn't, but she'd had an ugly bruise from where he'd smacked her.

When her mother had seen it, she'd raised hell, demanding her father fire Leon on the spot. Her father had refused, siding with his lieutenant. Half an hour later, her mother told her to pack, that they were leaving Mexico and going back to the States for good.

"Pack while I get our passports," her mom said. "I'll be back in twenty minutes."

But her mother had never come back.

According to her father, her mother had left on her own, only to change his story a few days later and say that one of his enemies had kidnapped her. Bristol had never believed either of those things. Her father had ordered Leon to kill her because he was the kind of man who couldn't stand the idea of someone taking something away from him, even if he didn't value it very much.

How could she not have known her father was such a horrible man?

In the other room, her father's cell phone rang, making her jump.

"Edein," her father greeted the caller. "I was just talking about you. Any idea when my shipment is arriving?"

"It should be docking in Manzanillo by the end of the week," a man's voice came over the speaker in an accented voice. Bristol wasn't sure, but it sounded Russian. "The ship is called the *Deliberate*."

She wondered absently if her father always put his phone on speaker when Leon was around. Then again, Leon was his right-hand man.

"And the missiles we discussed are part of this shipment?" her father asked, his voice firming on this detail. "For the money I'm paying, I expect those missiles to do exactly what you promised. They can take down a commercial aircraft, right?"

Bristol gasped, then quickly covered her mouth, afraid her father or Leon would hear. She hadn't given much thought to the kind of weapons her father had been talking about. She'd assumed he was buying more guns to go with the others his guards carried.

"I have a crew of men flying into the airport in Manzanillo," the Russian said. "Three of them for the administrative parts of finalizing the deal and discussing your next purchase. The fourth man will be a freelance agent Nick Chapman, who's currently working for me. He'll train your men in how to use the weapons."

Bristol silently groaned. More scumbag criminals hanging around the compound. Great.

"Chapman?" Her father's voice took on a decidedly curious tone.

Edein chuckled. "So you've heard of him? Not surprising. He has quite a reputation in our circles."

"Yes, I've heard a lot about him. Free-lance mercenary, arms dealer, security specialist. I can't wait to meet him. But I must warn you, if he is as impressive as I've heard, I intend to lure him away from you."

"Good luck with that my friend," Edein said with another laugh. "Nick works *with* me, not *for* me, and he is a difficult man to impress. If you're planning to make a run at him, you'll need to start with a hell of a lot of money and a beautiful woman. He has a definite weakness for both."

Bristol listened with half an ear to the rest of the conversation, wondering how long she was going to be trapped in the bathroom, when her father finally hung up. She hoped he and Leon would leave, but instead they hung around, talking cartel business in voices too low for her to make out much of what they were saying. That was okay. She wasn't interested anyway.

Sighing, she leaned back against the vanity. It was probably going to be a while, so she might as well get comfortable. Well, as comfortable as she could be hiding in a bathroom that her father or Leon could walk into any minute.

She was so lost in her thoughts she almost didn't hear the knock on the door of the study.

"Señor Muñoz! I didn't realize you were in here. Forgive me."

"That's all right, Isabella," her father said. "We

were finishing up anyway."

Isabella Rodriguez had been their house-keeper since Bristol was a little girl. Even though Isabella wasn't family, Bristol loved her like an aunt. If not for Isabella, Bristol probably would have gone insane in this prison. To say Isabella had been Bristol's rock after her mother had been murdered was an understatement.

She was still thinking about that when the door suddenly opened.

Bristol jumped, quickly backing away from the door and looking for somewhere to hide. Like she could get out of sight before whoever it was came in. How stupid was that?

Bristol held her breath, expecting to see her father or Leon, but instead it was Isabella, a stack of hand towels in her arm. Bristol sagged with relief. If there was one person in the villa she could trust, it was Isabella. Her friend gave a start, but didn't say anything. Instead, she changed out the old hand towels with new ones, then took a quick peek into her father's study.

"Your father and Leon just left," she whispered. "Stay here until I tell you it's safe to come out."

Bristol nodded, mouthing a silent, "Thank you."

Giving Bristol an exasperated look, Isabella turned and walked out, closing the door behind her.

Crap, that had been close.

No doubt Isabella thought Bristol had been in her father's study trying to figure out the combination to his safe again so she could get the passport he was keeping from her. Isabella had warned her to be careful about that. If her father or Leon ever found her...

Bristol shuddered. She didn't want to think what they'd do."

CHAPTER

Two

NASH ALWAYS WANTED TO VISIT MEXICO. BUT WHEN he pictured it, he'd envisioned a romantic getaway with a beautiful woman, days spent lying on the beach and nights exploring every inch of her body. Instead, he was in the port city of Manzanillo with Dalton and three federal agents neither of them had ever met, trying to understand what the hell they were both doing there. Two CIA agents sat in the front of the big SUV they were in, while an ATF agent occupied the third-row seat behind him and Dalton. None of the Feds seemed particularly interested in briefing them on the mission, but that didn't stop Nash from asking anyway.

In the passenger seat, Roman Bernard tossed him a quick glance over his shoulder. At least twenty years older than Nash, his hair was more gray than black, and he seemed to have a permanent furrow in his brow. Right now, he seemed to be more focused on the traffic in the crowded port city than anything else. It was getting close to sunset, and it looked like the man was having a hard time figuring out where he was going in the gathering dusk.

"Are you telling me nobody briefed you on this mission?" Roman frowned. "You're joking, right?"

Nash took a quick peek at the fed driving in the SUV, Charlie Shaw. Young enough to be Roman's son, he didn't seem nearly as concerned as the older agent about the route they were taking. But Shaw appeared to be as shocked that Nash and Dalton didn't know what was going on. Nash took a quick look at the ATF guy in the back seat and saw that Gerard Santiago was equally puzzled.

Unbelievable.

Nash took a deep breath and forced himself to let it out slowly so he wouldn't give into the urge to lean across the seat and punch Roman for being part of such a clueless organization. "Four nights ago, Dalton and I parachuted onto the deck of a cargo ship in the middle of the Pacific

Ocean with the other members of my SEAL Team and retrieved a crapload of missiles for you guys. After we went overboard with them, we spent nearly six hours floating around, getting our asses kicked by thirty-foot waves and being beat to shit by the missiles containers while we waited for a sub to pick us up. But instead of taking us back to San Diego, the sub dropped Dalton and me off on a resupply ship a few hours later. Some guy—who never bothered to tell us his name—shuffled us off to a helicopter and dropped us off in Mexico where another guy drove us to a cheap motel outside of Manzanillo. We've been sitting there ever since." He gave Roman a hard look. "So no, I'm not joking. And my sense of humor, which is normally one of my more endearing qualities, is pretty much gone at this point. Someone needs to start telling us what the hell is going on before Dalton and I decide we've had enough and leave."

In the front seat, Roman sighed and shook his head. "I'd like to say that what you're telling me was simply an oversight because this operation had to come together so fast. But the truth is, sometimes, the Agency can be a little too covert for its own good."

Admitting something like that must have been difficult for the fed to do, but that didn't mean Nash was ready to forgive and forget. "So, what's this about?"

"It's about those damn Russian missiles you found on that cargo ship," Roman said. "Headquarters at Langley decided they want to know what the plan is for them, as well as who the supplier is."

Nash wasn't surprised. But it still didn't explain why he and Dalton were involved.

"Okay, you have our attention," Nash said, speaking for both himself and Dalton. "What's the rest of the story?"

"The weapons shipment you and your team intercepted was heading for a man named Luis Munoz," Roman said, continuing to scan the city around them, like he was worried they were about to drive into an ambush or something. "As an upper-level lieutenant in the Amador cartel, Munoz is already a powerful man in the strongest crime organization in this part of the world, but it appears he's making a move up the ladder. This shipment of weapons is just the latest indication of how far he's willing to go."

"What the hell does a cartel crime boss want

with a shipment of surface-to-air missiles?" Nash asked.

He didn't know crap about how the Mexican drug cartels worked, but surface-to-air missiles seemed like a drastic escalation in firepower.

Shaw glanced at him in the rearview mirror. "When it looked like Munoz was bringing in a few automatic weapons and RPGs, we assumed he was planning to go after a police substation, maybe even a Mexican Army checkpoint. Something to raise his profile and beef up his reputation within the cartel. Then your team recovered the most expensive shoulder-fired weapons available in the world, and we started thinking he has something much bigger planned."

"Which is why the two of you are here," Santiago said from the back seat.

Nash turned to look at the guy. The ATF agent was probably only three or four years older than Shaw, but with his prematurely gray hair, heavily tattooed forearms, and a nose that looked like it had been broken multiple times, he looked a lot older. "We need to know what the hell Munoz is planning to do with those missiles. Just because we stopped him from getting this shipment doesn't mean he doesn't already have some. Or other weapons just as bad. We need to find out what his intentions are so we can decide if we need to step in to stop him."

Nash exchanged looks with Dalton. The subtext in the ATF agent's words had been clear. If Munoz was only going to be aiming these missiles at another member of the Amador cartel, Santiago and the others would likely back off and let it happen. Nash supposed he could understand that, but in a country as crowded as Mexico, it made him wonder how many innocent bystanders would end up getting hurt in that scenario.

"Just as importantly," Roman added with a pointed look at the ATF agent, "we'd like to figure out who Munoz was buying from. We know it has to be someone high up in the Russian Army, but we need to know exactly who it is, and whether they have any more of these missiles on the auction block."

Nash wondered what the hell they were leaving out, because it sure seemed like there was a ton of crap floating around unsaid in the background here.

"This is a thrilling story," Dalton told them, obviously getting the same feeling as Nash, "but you still haven't said what any of this has to do with us. We're Navy SEALs. We're good at swimming, parachuting, and running into and out of trouble. We don't usually play the secret agent game."

"No, you usually don't," Roman agreed. "But now you're going to get a chance to do it anyway. Because Nash happens to be a dead ringer for Nick Chapman."

"Who?" both Nash and Dalton asked at the same time.

"Nick Chapman, the weapons expert who flew into the Playa de Oro International Airport earlier this morning to train Munoz and his people on how to use the weapons he bought. I met him face to face for the first time at the airport when we snatched him and the other people coming in to finalize the deal, and it's not a stretch to say Nash could be the man's twin brother." Roman shrugged. "It also doesn't hurt that your military experiences are remarkably similar to his as well. Turns out Chapman used to be a SEAL before he was kicked out of the Navy and became a soldier of fortune and a key figure in the world of illegal arms trading."

Nash opened his mouth to ask how the hell the CIA just so happened to know he looked like some random arms-dealing soldier of fortune, but then decided he'd rather not know. He'd been involved with the Agency enough to know that many of the craziest conspiracy theories thrown around by the tin hat crowd had at least a sliver of truth to them. The idea that the CIA maintained a facial recognition database wasn't that far fetched in comparison to some of the crap he'd seen.

"I'm trying to keep up here, but you friggin' lost me," Nash said. Crap, he hated this covert stuff. That wasn't why he'd become a SEAL. "So, let's start with something simple. If I'm here because I look like Chapman, what's Dalton's part in this?"

Roman glanced at Dalton. "Truthfully, he wasn't supposed to be here. But your headquarters refused to allow a lone SEAL to take part in an operation like this. We had to take two of you or none of you. Basically, Dalton is your security. You brought him to watch your back because you don't trust us."

Dalton snorted. "Can't imagine why anyone would have a hard time believing that."

Nash silently agreed with Dalton, privately cheering the Navy Special Warfare Command. At least NSWC was looking out for their people.

"Okay, next question. Where are the weapons right now?"

"Still on the cargo ship carrying them pulled into port this morning. And before you ask, yes, we have the container in our possession. Along with the missiles you put on that Navy sub," Roman said. "Chapman and the other men were on the way to inspect the weapons when we grabbed them."

"If you have the weapons and this Chapman guy, I don't see why the hell you need us."

Roman let out a weary sigh. "Because Chapman isn't an arms dealer per se. He's more of a freelance middleman who works for some of the biggest arms dealers in the world, as well as a few organized crime syndicates and a handful of third-world dictators. His involvement doesn't tell us anything, other than the fact that this is a high-level operation."

"Hold on a second." Dalton frowned. "Are you seriously trying to tell me that with all your CIA resources, you can't figure out who he's working for? What about all of your enhanced interrogation techniques?"

Out of the corner of his eye, Nash caught Santiago's smirk behind them.

Roman shrugged. "Chapman and the other men who came here to facilitate the weapons transfer are being held in a safe house by the local police. We're questioning them, but so far, they're not talking. Which is why we're going with a different approach. One that needs you to pull off because Nick is the only one Munoz knows by reputation. He probably has a general idea what the man looks like and might have even talked to him."

That's when the pieces suddenly fell into place.

Nash ground his jaw. "Shit, you're planning for us to take the place of Chapman and his buddies in a meeting with Munoz. You think we can get him to slip up and reveal what his plans are for these missiles and who he bought them from."

"And you said SEALs were slow," Santiago muttered. "Seems like he understands the situation pretty well to me and apparently thinks the plan is as dumb as I do."

"Dumb?" Dalton snorted. "That's an understatement. Who could possibly think walking totally blind into a meeting with a Mexico cartel boss was a good idea? We're SEALs. We do more stupid stuff before nine AM than most people do all day. But even we'd never try anything this flaky. There are a dozen ways for this scheme to blow up in our faces."

Roman looked like he was about to argue, but Nash cut him off.

"Like how do you know that Munoz hasn't met Chapman in real life? Or any of the people the rest of you are supposed to be for that matter? Hell, it's the twenty-first century. What if he Skyped with Chapman? And have you ever thought that Munoz might have a mole inside the Mexican army? What if he already knows you arrested the real Chapman? We'd be dead within seconds of meeting with Munoz."

"Don't you think we've thought of all that?" Roman cursed. "Look, we don't have a choice, okay. We can't have some arms dealer out there selling high-tech missiles to anyone with a fat bank account. We have to find out who's behind this, and we need your help to do it."

Roman pointed Shaw toward an exit sign leading toward the beach before continuing. "While Chapman's work has taken him all over the world, there's no indication he's ever done business in Mexico. As for the rest of us, we're no-bodies sent here to oversee the deal and arrange for future purchases. There's absolutely no reason for Munoz to even consider we're not who we say we are."

"And the possibility of Munoz having a mole in the Mexican army?" Nash prodded, having a hard time not noticing how much of this plan was based on faith and pixie dust.

Shaw glanced at him in the rearview mirror. "The people we have watching Chapman and his crew are handpicked for their loyalty to the established government. Munoz won't learn about it from them."

Nash cursed silently, He'd been around a lot of *loyal* soldiers in his time spent working with foreign armies. They were rarely as loyal as they claimed.

"The people guarding Chapman and his crew don't have to keep this under wraps forever," Roman added. "They just have to give us a couple of days. The purpose of this meeting is to finalize the deal for the weapons and arrange for you to train Munoz's men how to use them. We'll get the information we need, then make the weapons hand-off, at which point the cavalry will be there to take Munoz into custody. Hopefully, we can do that in a day, two at the most."

"What if Munoz starts asking Nash some pointed questions?" Dalton asked. "About things he should know."

Roman hesitated. "We don't have any idea what the terms of the original deal were or what kind of arrangement Munoz has with Chapman, so Nash is going to have to wing most of that part of the conversation." He looked at Nash. "Trust me. You play your part and convince Munoz you're an expert in weapons, and I'll do everything I can to keep his attention focused on me."

Nash cursed silently. They were doing this regardless of how insane it was. "So, who's playing the part of the cavalry in this particular adventure?"

"The Mexican Army," Shaw answered.

Shit.

"We're here," Roman announced before Nash had a chance to once again point out that this was absolutely the worst plan ever.

Nash turned his attention to the open wrought iron gates ahead of them. The tall stucco perimeter walls on either side stretched off to the right and left as far as he could see. On the other side, the immense well-lit Spanish-style villa at the end of the paving stone lined driveway looked like it could comfortably house all eight sixteen-man platoons in SEAL Team 5.

But the hacienda didn't interest him as much as the guards patrolling the property. Four armed men stood at the gate they drove through, while three more lined the driveway. Five more were arrayed around the broad front steps of the home. Every one of them openly carried semi-automatic rifles as naturally as other people walked around with cell phones.

Shit just got real.

Shaw pulled into the large parking area that wrapped around the house to show off sweeping views of high bluffs and the jewel-like ocean beyond. A man in an impeccably cut suit descended the steps, but didn't come over to meet them. Instead, he stood there studying them with dark, unfathomable eyes. He had a thick mustache and jet-black hair even though he had to be nearing sixty.

Nash knew it was Luis Munoz without anyone telling him.

A big, muscular guy with dark hair and flat, emotionless eyes stood on Munoz's left. Everything about him screamed personal security.

It was the woman on the cartel boss's right

that caught and held Nash's attention. Tall with long, dark hair as black as Munoz's, her skin was light olive and absolutely perfect. But it was her eyes that captivated him. They were the most vivid, clear blue he'd ever seen.

Nash opened his mouth to ask Roman who she was, but the CIA agent spoke first.

"Before we kick off this mission, there are a few things I should tell you," he said, half turning in the front seat to look at Nash. "Chapman was kicked out of the Navy with a dishonorable discharge. He has a home in Brussels, but rarely stays there because he's too busy being a mercenary. He's also a player. You know, girl in every city kind of thing."

Nash cursed as Roman opened the door and stepped out. That information would have been nice to have before they rolled up on the cartel boss. The CIA agent shook Munoz's hand with a smile, clapping him on the shoulder as if they were best friends.

Beside Nash, Dalton chuckled as he reached for the door handle. "Nash Cantrell pretending to be a player. This should be interesting."

Nash would have laughed too if there was anything funny about it. Cursing under his breath, he put on his game face, then opened the door and stepped out of the SUV. He had to nail this or they were all dead.

But as Munoz walked over to meet him, Nash remembered something Roman had said about Chapman being from Brussels. Damn, he didn't know the first thing about Brussels. Of all the places he'd been in the world, Belgium wasn't one of them.

"Señor Chapman." Munoz held out his hand. "Your reputation precedes you. I have heard much about you."

Nash smiled. "All good, I trust."

Munoz laughed. "Indeed." He glanced at the raven-haired woman still standing near the steps. "Come meet our guest, my dear."

She glared at Munoz, her blue eyes like ice as she slowly made her way over to them.

"My daughter, Bristol," Munoz introduced.

Nash did a double take. *Daughter?* He'd assumed she was the cartel boss's wife.

He opened his mouth to say something witty and charming, but when she lifted her gaze to meet his, he was so mesmerized, it was all he could do to offer his hand.

If Bristol noticed how tongue-tied he was,

she didn't let on. But that was only because she was too busy looking at him like he was something she'd just scraped off the bottom of her shoe. Nash half expected her to wipe her palm off on the curve-hugging wrap dress she wore after shaking his hand. Damn. They'd just met and she already hated him.

How much worse could this mission get?

"Not hungry?" Nick Chapman asked.

Bristol turned her head to look at him. She still couldn't believe her father had pimped her out to this piece of crap. But not five minutes after she'd sneaked out of his office, he'd intercepted her on the way to the library and informed her that she'd be joining him and his guests for dinner. The idea of sitting at the same table with her father was bad enough, but when he'd told her that he wanted her to "be nice to Nick Chapman and show him a good time" so the arms dealer would be more open to a job offer, she'd almost punched him.

"I'm your daughter, not a prostitute," she'd

snapped. "If you want someone to entertain the arms dealer, hire one of them."

Thinking that was the end of it, she'd tried to walk away, but her father grabbed her arm, almost yanking her off her feet.

"That's right, you *are* my daughter. Which means you'll damn well do as I told you and entertain Nick Chapman."

"If I don't?" she'd demanded. "What are you going to do? Murder me like you did my mother?"

The words were out before she could stop them, and from the look of rage on her father's face, she thought he'd do exactly that. But he merely tightened his grip on her arm and regarded her coldly.

"If you don't, I'll say yes the next time Leon asks me for your hand in marriage," her father said.

She'd tried not to flinch...and failed. If she refused to play nice, her father would give her to Leon without a second thought. That would be a fate worse than death.

"It's your choice," her father added, knowing he'd already won. "Make it quickly."

Giving in had nearly crushed her spirit, and Bristol hated herself for nodding. In this case however, she was willing to go with the evil she didn't know over the one she did. With his dark hair, rugged features and chocolate brown eyes, Nick was undoubtedly easier on the eyes than Leon, especially in the black suit he'd changed into for dinner, but she was still withholding her judgment as to whether his company was better than her father's hired muscle.

On the other side of Nick, blond-haired Dalton regarded them curiously. From the smile tugging at the corner of his mouth, she was certain he'd heard Nick's question. She wasn't sure what was so funny about it.

The three men who'd arrived with Nick and Dalton weren't nearly as interested in what she and the arms dealer were talking about. Neither were the four other men at the table. Then again, they were regulars at the villa, a sordid collection of lawyers and accountants who had something to do with keeping her father out of jail—and a grave. There were a handful of guards in the dining room as well posted at various places, but they couldn't care less about her. From where he stood behind her father, Leon, on the other hand, was staring daggers at her and Nick. Bristol ignored him.

"Not really," she said in answer to Nick's question.

She belatedly remembered to paste a fake smile on her face in case her father happened to glance their way from the far end of the table, something he did every few minutes when he wasn't deep in conversation with the man named Roman. She was a little surprised her father was openly discussing a weapons deal in front of her. It was another indication of how far gone he was. Clearly, he no longer cared that she knew he was in the cartel.

Nick regarded the plate of food in front of her for a moment, then looked at her again. "I hope it's not because of the company?"

She'd been waiting for Nick to start making a move on her at some point. She'd heard enough of her father's phone conversation with Edein to know the arms dealer was a player. But what he'd just asked didn't sound like any kind of come-on line she'd ever heard.

She threw a covert glance in her father's direction to see if he was listening, but he was still too engrossed in negotiations to bother with her at the moment. Leon must have heard, though. He looked so furious she thought he might bite his tongue off. Then again, maybe he was simply furious he was talking to another man. Maybe she'd get lucky and he'd choke on that tongue when it fell off.

"Of course not." She gave Nick a smile. "Why would you think that?"

Nick shrugged. "I saw your face when we arrived. I got the feeling you weren't thrilled to see us."

She opened her mouth to deny it, but Nick cut her off with a chuckle that was way sexier than it had a right to be.

"Don't worry about it," he said. "If I were you, I wouldn't want to have dinner with mercenaries, arms dealers, and criminals either."

Bristol blinked. If she didn't know better, she'd think he meant that. But that didn't make sense considering he was one of the aforementioned mercenary, arms dealing criminals.

"If you missed it, that was Nick trying to put you at ease," Dalton said, leaning forward to grin at her. "You probably missed it though because he sucks when it comes to being charming."

Nick frowned at the blond man. "Was anyone talking to you?"

"No. But since it's my job to keep you safe, I

figured I should step in and help translate your clumsy attempts at being suave before you trip over your tongue and hurt yourself."

Shaking his head, Nick turned back to her. "Ignore Dalton. He has a hard time remembering why I hired him. He's paid to take a bullet for me, not criticize me."

Bristol couldn't help smiling. She might not know Nick well, but there was no mistaking the easy camaraderie between the two men. They were more like friends than employer and employee.

"It's okay. I'm used to it," she said. "My father is in the Amador cartel. I have dinner with killers and drug dealers every night."

That wasn't quite true since she never ate dinner with her father, but they lived in the same house, which was close enough for her.

Nick's dark eyes danced as he studied her. "Ouch. So, you're comparing me with killers and drug dealers now?"

She laughed. To say Nick wasn't anything like she expected was an understatement. Maybe he was just working her, but if so, he was damn good at it.

"Okay, maybe you're a little better than that,"

she said.

Out of the corner of her eye, she caught her father looking at them. Her smile faltered a little. She didn't want him getting too pleased with himself.

Nick must have realized her father was watching them, too. "Forgive me if I'm overstepping, but I couldn't help noticing your father made sure we sat together. What's the deal with that?"

As he waited for an answer, he casually turned his attention to the shrimp-filled enchiladas on his plate. Nick might seem like a nice guy, but there was a good chance that anything she said would make it back to her father. Did she really need more trouble like that?

Some part of her must have thought she did—or didn't care—because after taking a few bites of her own enchilada she found herself answering his question.

"My father plans on offering you a job and insists you'll be more inclined to take it if I'm nice to you."

Out of the corner of her eye, she saw Nick stiffen, the fork he held hovering above his plate for a few seconds. Even Dalton had become motionless. Bristol hadn't even realized he was still eavesdropping on their conversation.

Nick slowly set down his fork and looked at her, his eyes unreadable. "Your father wants you to flirt with me just so I'll be more willing to work for him?"

She might not have been able to read his expression, but she definitely picked up on the tension in his voice. He genuinely seemed shocked. Maybe even angry. She wondered why. It wasn't like she was anything to him.

"You apparently don't know my father very well," she said bitterly. "If you did, you wouldn't be so surprised at the lengths he'll go to to get what he wants."

Nick locked eyes with her, his dark gaze intense. "If I don't take him up on his offer, will he blame you?"

Bristol stared at him, too stunned to do more than that. Why was he acting like he cared about her? Some small, almost childlike voice in the back of her mind whispered that Nick's concern might be real. That if she was honest with him, he might somehow help her get away from her father and out of this horrible situation.

But then reality intruded, and the

cynical part of her that had taken over the day she learned Luis Munoz wasn't the man she'd thought he was pointed out that Nick wasn't any kind of saint. He was an arms dealer here to sell illegal weapons to her father. A man who made his money selling instruments of war to anyone who could pay for them. He was playing her by making it seem like he cared about her so it would be easier to get in her panties.

Well, she wasn't falling for it.

Bristol broke eye contact and concentrated on her dinner plate, taking a few more bites of enchilada before taking a sip of wine.

"Did I hear my father say that you live in Brussels?" she asked, setting down her glass.

Nick did a double take at the sudden change in conversation. In a weird way, his reaction made her almost feel like she'd regained a bit of control over the situation. Like she'd caught him at his game and now she was the one calling the shots. It was probably juvenile but her life hadn't been hers to control for over a year. Even a tiny step in the right direction felt good.

He finally nodded. "Yeah. I have a place in Brussels, but my work keeps me on the move so much, I can't remember the last time I was there.

In fact, sometimes it feels like I've never even been to Brussels at all. I love Europe, though. You can drive a few hours in any one direction and the scenery changes. There's something magical about that."

Bristol cursed silently. She'd been so quick to talk about something other than her father that she'd said the first thing that had popped into her head. Unfortunately, asking Nick about his home in Europe had only brought up another sensitive topic—the fact that she was a prisoner here and that all the dreams she'd once had of traveling and seeing the world were dead and gone.

"Have you ever been to Europe?" Nick asked.

She shook her head sadly. Her mother had urged her to take a year off in between her bachelors and masters programs and see the world, but she'd wanted to get her schooling done first, figuring she'd travel afterward.

Things obviously hadn't worked out the way she'd planned

Isabella was the only other person she ever talked to about it but suddenly she found herself wanting to tell Nick, too. Dammit, why did his deep, sexy voice make her want to confide in him about stuff she shouldn't?

"No, I've never been there," she admitted softly. "I've always wanted to go, but never had the chance. Actually, I've never been outside Mexico except to go to college."

"Where'd you go?"

"Connecticut."

"Really?" He grinned. "I've never been there. What's it like?"

She smiled at the memory. "Beautiful, even if it was too cold most of the time. The snow was brutal for a girl from Mexico."

Nick chuckled, the husky sound making her feel warm all over. Had she really thought he'd been playing her before? The whole idea suddenly seemed kind of silly.

"What'd you think the first time you saw the white stuff?" he asked, leaning in a little closer.

Regardless of whether his interest was genuine or not, it was fun thinking back to that first magical moment she'd felt snow on her face and seen it blanketing the campus of Central Connecticut State University. Her father forgotten for the moment, she told Nick about building a snowman with her friends and getting in a snowball fight with what seemed like the entire student body, then making snow angels afterward. As they talked, all the misery that had been weighing her down for so long simply disappeared and she was almost happy again. It'd been so long she'd forgotten what it felt like.

Then her father appeared at her side. He rested one hand on her shoulder, making her jump.

"I knew you two would hit it off," he said with a laugh.

There was no laughter in his eyes though. Just cold calculation. Any happiness she'd felt a few moments ago disappeared immediately. Bristol attempted to shrug his hand off her shoulder, but he tightened his grip ever so slightly.

"And since my weapons won't be off the ship until the day after tomorrow, Nick has some free time until then," her father continued. "Which makes it the perfect opportunity for the two of you to get to know each other better, my dear."

Bristol opened her mouth to tell her she was busy the next day, and every day after for the foreseeable future, but Nick spoke first.

"I'm sure your daughter has better things to do than spend time with me." Nick's eyes never left hers. "I can keep myself occupied."

"Don't be silly," her father said firmly. "In

fact, I insist you and my daughter take my yacht out tomorrow."

Nick considered that. "Only if Bristol agrees."

"Of course, she agrees." Her father squeezed her shoulder again. "Don't you, my dear?"

She almost told her father to go to hell, but then caught herself. This was the first time since her mother's death that he was allowing her to leave the villa. True, it was only so she could entertain his precious arms dealer, and while it might not be easy to slip away from the guards her father would almost certainly send with them, she'd put up with Nick if it meant getting a chance to escape.

So, she nodded. "Of course."

"Excellent." Her father smiled at Nick. "*Lydia's Dream* is a beautiful yacht, Nick. Almost as beautiful as the woman she's named after— Bristol's mother, rest her soul. I know she'd be very pleased the two of you are going to take it out and enjoy yourselves. She loved that boat almost as much as she loved Bristol and me."

Bristol stiffened. Her father hadn't so much as whispered her mother's name since he'd murdered her—or had someone do it for him. Hearing it roll of his tongue like he was trying to sell Nick a damn used car made her so furious she wanted to scream.

She stared down at her nearly full plate, hoping if she focused on something besides her father that she wouldn't give in to the urge to grab a gun from the nearest guard and shoot him with it. But then she saw the steak knife beside her plate and realized how much easier it would be to simply plunge it into her father's heart instead.

She was just reaching for it when she felt Nick's hand on her thigh underneath the table. She had no idea how he'd known what she was about to do, but the contact was enough to jerk her out of the rage she was in and help her get a grip.

That didn't mean she was going to sit there and listen to her father talk about her mother anymore.

Shoving her father's hand away, she shot to her feet, pushing her chair back so hard it almost toppled over. Turning, she headed for the door, refusing to look at him or anyone else in the room. Not even Nick.

"Bristol," her father said sharply. "Where are you going?"

She didn't answer. She didn't stop walking either. She couldn't. Not if she wanted to keep it together and hold back the tears that threatened to run down her cheeks right there in front of everyone.

CHAPTER

Three

BRISTOL MADE ONE HELL OF AN EXIT AS SHE WALKED out of the lavish dining room. Not surprising, Nash thought. She was an extremely captivating woman. One who'd figuratively just kicked her father in the balls in front of his guests.

Nash couldn't blame her. Munoz had practically served her up on a silver platter for him—or rather, Nick Chapman. What the hell kind of father did that?

But while that was definitely reason enough for Bristol to resent the man, it wasn't until Munoz mentioned her mother that her whole demeanor changed. If Nash hadn't put his hand on her leg, she probably would have actually tried to stab the cartel boss with that steak knife she'd been reaching for.

Munoz stared at the door, a stunned

expression on his face like he was shocked his daughter had left. After a moment, his face hardened and he looked at Leon, some silent communication passing between them. Munoz's right-hand muscle nodded once then strode from the room.

Nash cursed silently. He wasn't sure what Munoz had told Leon to do, but his gut told him it wasn't anything good. Bristol had embarrassed Munoz. That wasn't a good thing even if she was his daughter.

"Stay here," he whispered to Dalton.

Tossing his napkin on the table, Nash pushed back his chair and followed Leon. Dalton was damn good to have in a firefight, no doubt about it, but this had the potential to get sticky fast. If things went bad, he'd rather have Dalton here keeping an eye on Munoz and the other guards.

Two of them immediately moved to intercept Nash. He gave them a hard look, silently begging them to try and stop him. Both men glanced over his shoulder in Munoz's direction, clearly waiting for the cartel boss to tell them what to do. A moment later, they stepped aside. Obviously, Munoz didn't seem to mind if he got into it with Leon.

Nash wondered what that was about.

Once outside the dining room, Nash saw

Leon disappear around the corner at the end of the hallway. Nash jogged after him even as a part of his head wanted to know what the hell he was doing. He was supposed to be here playing the part of a criminal and getting information about Russian arms dealers out of Luis Munoz. He wasn't here to play the hero and rescue the damsel in distress. Especially when that damsel in distress happened to be the daughter of the man they were trying to put in prison.

That didn't keep him from going after Bristol anyway.

The hallway led to a state-of-the-art kitchen big enough to park a few cars in. Bristol was on the far side of the room near a huge stainless-steel refrigerator, Leon towering over her menacingly. The asshole had a hand wrapped around her wrist and was saying something low and threatening sounding in Spanish. Nash had picked up enough of the language since becoming a SEAL and moving to San Diego to know Leon was saying she belonged to him.

Anger surged through Nash. No friggin' way was he going to stand by and watch any woman get abused, and Leon looked like he was half a second away from smacking Bristol.

Out of the corner of his eye, Nash noticed an older woman standing with her back to the stove, terror on her face. Ignoring her, he strode across the kitchen.

"Let Bristol go," Nash ordered.

Bristol jumped, clearly surprised by Nash's presence, but the relief in her eyes was obvious. If Leon was stunned, he didn't let on. Instead, he stabbed Nash with a murderous look.

"You should go back to the dining room," Leon suggested in a low voice. "This is between her and me. It's none of your business."

Nash stopped a few feet away. "I'm making it my business."

Leon muttered something in Spanish under his breath and tightened his grip on Bristol's arm, nearly jerking her off her feet as he pulled her closer. Nash would have preferred to get Bristol away from Leon before things got ugly, but that might not be possible.

Nash tensed, ready to dive for Leon's left knee when the man shoved Bristol roughly aside, sending her stumbling across the kitchen. The older woman by the stove darted forward and caught Bristol before she crashed to the floor, then dragged her to the other side of the room out of harm's way.

Nash barely had time to blink before Leon came at him swinging. Nash cursed. As much as he wanted to wipe the floor with the buffoon, he didn't want to damage the guy seriously. He might deserve an ass whooping of epic proportions for putting his hands on Bristol, but putting Munoz's personal bodyguard in the hospital wasn't likely to help when it came to getting the info they were here for.

He ducked under Leon's arm, driving a fist into the man's exposed stomach before quickly backpedaling. Leon grunted, but immediately came at him again. Nash slowed him with a quick jab to the jaw then a punch to the ribs.

Leon bellowed in rage as Nash darted away into clear space. There was a lot of frustration in that sound, but some pain there, too.

Nash glanced to the side, hoping the two women had been smart and gotten the hell out of the kitchen. But no, Bristol and the older woman were still there. Bristol seriously looked like she wanted a piece of Leon. In fact, the older woman had to physically hold her back. Damn, Munoz's daughter was ballsy. Maybe too ballsy for her own good.

He turned back to Leon, expecting the bodyguard to take another swing at him, but the man was headed for the large marble island in the middle of the kitchen. Nash wasn't sure what he was up to until Leon jerked a big chef's knife out of a rack of blades.

Shit.

Nash had been willing to play this out for the sake of the mission, even if all he really wanted to do was beat the crap out of the guy. But now that Leon had a weapon, all bets were off. He wouldn't hesitate to kill this asshole.

"You're going to look fucking stupid with that knife sticking out of your ass," Nash told him.

Leon laughed, holding the knife low and away. Like a man who knew what he was doing with a blade.

Nash dropped into a defensive stance, waiting for Leon's first move, when a low male voice intruded from the doorway.

"Leon, the boss wants you."

Nash didn't have to look to know it was one of Munoz's guards. For some reason, the cartel boss wanted to put a stop to the fight before it was over.

Leon didn't seem eager to leave, but another

sharp reminder from the other man finally broke through the fury. He pointed the tip of his knife at Nash. "This isn't over," he muttered.

Tossing the chef's blade onto the island with a clatter, he threw an angry look in Bristol's direction, then walked out of the kitchen. The other guard followed.

Nash looked at Bristol. "You okay?"

"Yes," she said, the little quiver in her voice the only indication of how scared she really was. "Thank you. For helping me, I mean."

He nodded. "You're welcome."

"And while I'm grateful, it was stupid of you to do it," she added.

"Bristol!" the older woman scolded.

"You know I'm right, Isabella," Bristol said then looked at Nash. "Leon is a sociopath. He would have killed you with that knife without giving it a thought."

"He would have tried," Nash corrected, then shrugged. "We all do stupid things, but in my defense, I have to admit I have a hard time thinking straight when I'm around a beautiful woman."

Bristol sighed. "You don't have to shower me with compliments. I already thanked you."

He grinned. "Who said I talking about you?

Maybe I was talking about Isabella."

The older woman blushed but laughed. "I think you need to be careful around this one, Bristol. Something tells me that he might be more dangerous than Leon." She regarded Nash thoughtfully. "But Bristol is right about Leon, Señor Chapman. Watch yourself around him. He'll stab you in the back given the chance."

"I'll keep that in mind," Nash promised then looked at Bristol. "Are you going to be okay tonight? Do I need to worry about Leon coming back to bother you?"

Bristol studied him for a long time with those mesmerizing blue eyes of hers. A man could lose himself in that perfect gaze. "I don't think Leon will try anything else tonight. He only came after me because my father allowed it. And my father only did that to see what you would do."

He did a double take. "Why?"

"Because my father is a very manipulative man." She gave Nash a small smile. "Thank you for worrying about me."

Nash opened his mouth to tell her it wasn't a big deal, but the way Bristol was gazing at him tied up his tongue in a knot.

"Good night," she said.

"Good night."

Giving him a nod, she left the room, Isabella at her heels. The two of them might think Leon was the dangerous one around here, but from Nash's perspective, Bristol was the one he was going to have to watch out for.

Someone knocked on the door of Nash's bedroom before he'd had a chance to do more than wander around and locate the bathroom. But hey, that was still an accomplishment. The bedroom Munoz had given him to use was larger than his entire apartment back in San Diego. Hell, the bathroom by itself would have swallowed his whole living room.

As he reached for the doorknob, Nash wondered if it was Leon with a big ass knife in his hand ready to pick up where he'd left off. He was almost disappointed when he saw it was Dalton and Roman. Years of experience as a Navy SEAL told him that he and Leon were going to fight at some point. Nash would rather get it over with so he could have a good night's sleep.

He opened the door wider, motioning them in. "I was wondering when you two would show up."

Nash hadn't gotten a chance to talk to either of them after his little run-in with Leon. No doubt they wanted to know what the hell had happened in the kitchen, and why Leon had spent the rest of the evening staring daggers at Nash. But before he could even open his mouth, Roman held up an index finger up to his lips and shook his head.

Taking a black box the size of a cell phone out from an inner pocket of his suit jacket, Roman slowly moved around the room, poking his head— and the box—under and around every nook and cranny in the place. Bed, couches, dressers, lamps, TV—even the air conditioner vents and ceiling fans. Only after he'd gone around every corner of the three-room suite *twice* did Roman tuck the box back in his pocket and give them a nod.

"It's clean."

Dalton frowned. "You seriously think Munoz would bug his own house? Damn, you've been doing this too long. You're getting paranoid."

"Hell, yeah, I'm paranoid." Roman snorted. "And it's the only thing that's kept me alive doing this damn job so I keep doing it."

Nash couldn't help but notice the bitter tone in the man's voice and would have asked him why the hell he kept doing *this damn job* if he hated it so much, but Roman spoke first.

"So, what was that shit with you and Munoz's personal security guard?" he asked bluntly, coming to stand in front of Nash. The expression on his face made it clear he wasn't happy. "You realize how bad things would have gone if you'd screwed up and killed Leon, right? Failing the mission would have been the least of our problems. Munoz probably would have murdered us all."

Nash chuckled. "Glad to hear you were never worried about me being able to handle Leon."

"I couldn't care less if he'd have killed you," Roman snapped. "That wouldn't have endangered the mission nearly as much as the other way around. Might have even helped it because it would have forced Munoz to accept the weapons without a demonstration."

"Good to know you've got my back," Nash muttered dryly. He was surprised at the CIA agent's complete lack of concern when it came to his life. Even Dalton seemed shocked. "But as it turns out, you don't have to worry about Munoz getting pissed about the fight. He purposely set things in motion to make sure Leon and I went at it."

Roman eyed him doubtfully. "What makes you say that?"

"It turns out that he wants me to work for him." Nash shrugged. "Hell, he basically pimped his daughter out to me as a fringe benefit."

Just saying those words out loud pissed Nash off all over again. Roman, on the other hand, merely looked calculating.

"What does he have to gain pitting you against his right-hand man?" the agent asked.

"I don't know for sure yet," Nash admitted. "But if I had to guess, I'd say it was a test to see if I'm a suitable replacement for Leon."

Dalton crossed his arms over his chest. "What does his daughter think of her part in the recruitment?"

"I'm pretty sure she's not thrilled with it," Nash said. Though it definitely explained why she'd looked at him like she hated him when they first got to the villa. "But something tells me that Munoz doesn't care what his daughter thinks."

Roman began pacing the room, a thoughtful expression on his face. "This job offer concept could really work for us." He glanced at Nash, but his eyes were focused on a spot a hundred miles away as his mind apparently worked through the covert math. "You getting with Munoz's daughter has some serious potential. From what I saw, she seemed to connect with you during dinner. And after you ran to her rescue, I'm willing to bet she's even more into you. Do you think you can work the daughter? Maybe on that yacht tomorrow? Use her to get an inside track on the info we need on her father?"

Nash ground his jaw. He wanted to point out that *the daughter* had a name and wasn't guilty of any crimes simply because her father was a dirtbag. But he kept his opinion to himself and gave Roman a noncommittal shrug.

"Maybe."

Roman nodded. "Good. I'm meeting Munoz later tonight. He wants to talk about another weapons deal. Something bigger than surface-to-air missiles this time. If I get a chance, I'll explore this rift with his daughter and see if there's anything we can use."

"Careful with that," Nash said as Roman headed for the door. "Bristol won't be of any help to us if you alert Munoz to what we're trying to do."

Hand on the doorknob, the CIA agent looked over his shoulder at him and Dalton. "I've been playing these games since the two of you were in diapers. You worry about the woman. I'll handle her daddy."

With that, Roman walked out, leaving them standing there staring at each other in disbelief.

"He's not that old, is he?" Dalton asked. "Or do we just look that young?"

Nash shrugged and walked over to collapse on one of the two expensive leather couches in the living room. Crap, it had been a long friggin' day.

"I might be wrong about this, but I get the feeling you aren't thrilled with the idea of using Bristol to get dirt on her dad," Dalton said, unbuttoning his jacket and taking a seat on the other couch.

As his friend leaned back and stretched out an arm on either side of him, Nash caught sight of the underarm holster rig Dalton wore...and the large Glock automatic nestled neatly inside it.

"Where'd you get the tactical Tupperware?" he asked. "Because you sure as hell didn't have it when we showed up today."

"This?" Dalton asked, motioning at the gun and the three extra magazines in a holder on his belt. "I was schmoozing with a few of Munoz's guards earlier and when I mentioned that I'm your bodyguard, they were nice enough to let me borrow it.

Professional courtesy, I guess." His friend pinned him with a look. "And if you think you distracted me with that question, you didn't. What's going on with Bristol? I heard the two of you talking at dinner, and I saw your face when Leon went after her. You were in full-on SEAL mode and ready to kick some ass."

Nash didn't bother to deny it. He and Dalton were closer than most brothers. The guy would know in a second if he were lying. "She was in trouble. I went to help."

"You like her," Dalton said flatly. "Four hours after meeting the daughter of the cartel boss we're supposed to help send to prison and you're in love."

"I just met her, so how the hell could I be in love, doofus?" Nash leaned back, running his hand through his hair with a sigh. "Look, Bristol is in a shitty situation. Having a dad who's a dirtbag doesn't automatically make her guilty by association, you know."

"Yeah, I know," Dalton said. "But you don't think she might be playing you? Saying exactly what she thinks you want to hear to get what she wants?"

"It's possible," Nash agreed. "But aren't we doing the same thing?"

"Yeah, but we're the good guys."

Nash replayed the day's events through his head. Between getting pulled into a CIA operation they knew absolutely nothing about and running a sting that involved putting dangerous weapons in the hands of a cartel boss, to playing games with a woman's life and working with a fed who'd practically admitted he couldn't care less if Nash and Dalton got killed in the process as long as the case ran smoothly, none of those things struck him as something the good guys would do.

"You sure about that?" he asked Dalton.

CHAPTER

I CAN'T REMEMBER THE LAST TIME I SAW YOU IN A BATHING suit," Isabella said.

Bristol glanced down at the simple black one-piece barely visible under the cover-up as she and Isabella walked down the stone steps leading from the villa down to the pier where the yacht was waiting for them. Isabella was right. It had been a while since she'd worn one.

"I sure as hell wasn't going to wear one hanging around the pool so my father's guards could ogle me," she said.

Isabella carefully held onto the railing as she moved down the steps. "But you're wearing one today."

"Because I'm going out on a boat," Bristol reminded her, wondering why this was even a topic of conversation. It wasn't like she was wearing a skimpy bikini. She probably wouldn't even take off the cover up. "What else would I wear?"

"That's very practical of you." A smile curved the corners of Isabella's lips. "No chance that a certain attractive and charming American might also have something to do with your choice of clothing?"

Bristol opened her mouth to deny it but stopped herself. Isabella knew her too well to try lying to her. She'd call Bristol on it in a second. Not that Bristol would lie to her. Isabella had always been like a second mother to her, and since her real mother's disappearance, the woman had done everything she could do protect Bristol from her father.

All that said, Bristol wasn't exactly sure how to put the answer to Isabella's question into words. While her father had demanded she "be nice" to Nick, he hadn't told her what to wear. She'd made that decision completely her own. Partly because of Nick. And partly because if she somehow managed to escape she couldn't swim in the jeans and T-shirt hidden in the bottom of her tote in a waterproof bag. But Isabella didn't know about her escape plan.

"It's complicated," she finally admitted as

they reached the dock and made their way toward the large yacht moored at the end.

Like almost everything her father owned, *Lydia's Dream* was expensive and opulent. But since many of her fondest memories of her mother included this boat, Bristol ignored her father's habit of over-the-top displays of his criminal wealth this once.

There were two guards waiting for them at the bottom of the gangway and two more already on the yacht. No doubt they were on board to keep a close eye on her and report back to her father. Thankfully, Leon was nowhere in sight.

"Anything involving a man usually is," Isabella said with a laugh. "But in this case, I think the situation is probably simpler than you're making it out to be. Señor Chapman is a very attractive man who's clearly interested in you. He's also the first man you've ever met willing to stand up to your father and his guards. You're intrigued and want him to know it."

Bristol lifted a brow behind her sunglasses. "By wearing a bathing suit?"

"Women are blessed with the knowledge that men are clueless when it comes to recognizing any kind of subtle hint. So, we've had to develop alternative methods to let them know we're interested in them. Flashing some cleavage and showing off a lot of leg is just one of the ways to tell a man that."

Bristol stopped halfway up the gangplank to gape at Isabella. "I can't believe you just said that."

Isabella waved a hand. "Just because I don't have any children of my own doesn't mean I don't understand how the process works. In fact, I'm quite good at that part of it. I'm simply giving you the benefit of my experience with men, if you care to take advantage of it."

Bristol shook her head. Clearly, there was a side of Isabella that she didn't know very much about. "You know I always want your advice, but none of that applies to Nick and me. He's an arms dealer my father is trying to recruit into the cartel, not boyfriend material."

Isabella nudged her further up the gangway. "Perhaps. Do you mind if I ask you a simple question then?"

Bristol wasn't so sure that was a good idea since there was no telling what was going to come out of Isabella's mouth next, but she nodded anyway. "Okay."

"What was the last thing you remember

thinking about before you fell asleep last night?" Isabella asked, stepping aboard the yacht.

Bristol almost said she didn't remember, but then she screwed up and actually thought about the question. She blushed as an image of a bare-chested Nick came to mind.

Isabella laughed. "I thought so. Don't worry, I'm not judging," she added when Bristol started to protest. "As I said, Señor Chapman is a very attractive man."

She shoved the image of the half-dressed arms dealer out of her head, which was a rather difficult task. "Assuming for the sake of argument that you're right and I am interested in Nick, wouldn't it be easier to simply tell him that?"

Then what? They'd live happily ever after? Not likely since she intended to make a run for the border that afternoon.

Beside her, Isabella was staring at her like she was dense. "Oh, dear child, if you tell a man what you want, there's no incentive on his part to keep working hard. He'll expect you to make everything easy on him, and then where would you be?"

"Perhaps together," a gruff voice said from

behind them.

Bristol turned to see an older man with a head of shaggy, salt and pepper hair, a heavy mustache, and skin tanned dark from years in the sun. He cracked a smile the moment he saw her, and Bristol found herself running over to hug him.

"Alejandro! It's been so long since I've seen you."

The captain of *Lydia's Dream* beamed at her. "Too long. But you are here now and that's all that matters. Though you shouldn't let Isabella fill your head with crazy talk of making life hard for someone you're interested in. Take an old man's word for it, when two people play games with each other, they both lose."

Isabella laughed. "Says the man who doesn't like to work hard for anything. Who are you going to believe, Bristol? The woman who helped raise you or the man who only loves his boat."

Bristol could only smile as the two old friends traded barbs with each other. Isabella and Alejandro had flirted with each other as long as she could remember. Bristol had always assumed it was all in fun, but looking at them now, she wasn't so sure.

She was reminding herself to ask Isabella about it later when movement on the dock caught her eye. Bristol turned to see Nick and Dalton coming their way. Other than noting that his bodyguard was dressed in a suit like her father's guards, Bristol had a hard time seeing anything but the subject of her earlier conversation with Isabella.

Nick was wearing a pair of black swim trunks and a tank top. Bristol wasn't sure which she appreciated more, his lean, muscled legs or the broad shoulders, bulging biceps, and the hint of serious pecs and abs hiding under his shirt. Maybe Isabella was onto something when she suggested Bristol was intrigued by him. It wasn't just the obvious physical attributes that did it for her either—though there were a lot to be impressed with. It was also the confident way he walked as well as the casual way he laughed and joked with his bodyguard, as if being in crazy situations like he was in at the moment was a normal part of his life.

"That is one extremely handsome man," Isabella said softly from beside her. "I can see why a woman might dream about him as she drifted off to sleep."

Bristol turned and saw that they were alone on the deck. "You shouldn't be saying stuff like that out loud," she teased. "What if Alejandro overheard? He might get jealous."

Isabella smiled. "One can only hope."

CHAPTER

I DON'T MIND WAITING ON BRISTOL," DALTON SAID, placing two glasses of champagne on the polished teak table in front of them and giving her a smile he probably thought was charming before looking at Nash. "But if you want anything else, you can get it yourself. I'm paid to take a bullet for you, not bring you drinks."

In reality, Nash supposed that was true enough. But having his buddy at his beck and call was pretty damn entertaining even if it was only for show.

"Okay," Nash said. "But there goes that expensive Christmas present I was planning to buy for you."

Dalton snorted. "Well, damn. I guess I'll have to go out and buy that Old Spice gift set all on my own then."

"Have it your way," Nash called out as his teammate disappeared down the steps that led to the galley. "But that gift set is going to run you almost thirty dollars and you could have had it for free."

Beside him, Bristol laughed. "I can't believe your bodyguard talks to you like that."

"Tell me about it," Nash muttered. "I'd fire him, but he's like family so I'm stuck with him."

Bristol sipped her champagne, eyes sparkling in the sun sneaking into the half covered deck area where they sat on comfortable bench seats. He'd pulled off his shirt after the big yacht had left the dock, and Bristol had followed suit, taking off her cover-up. He'd done his very best not to stare, but it'd been damn hard. She had a spectacular body. The sleek, high-cut one-piece showed off her generous curves and revealed legs so long he'd found himself daydreaming more than once about how many hours it would take him to lick every inch of them.

"Why would you want to fire him?" she asked, setting down her glass with a smile. "I think it's great the two of you are close enough to rib each other. None of my father's guards even talk to him, much less tease him."

He put on a shocked expression. "You mean Leon and your father don't go barhopping together?"

Bristol laughed again. Nash couldn't decide what he liked better, the way she did it or the way a certain part of her anatomy jiggled just right *when* she did.

Okay, that was a lie. He definitely knew which one he liked more. But he was smart enough to refrain from thinking about her perfect breasts too much. Unless he wanted to pitch a tent in his swim trucks. Which he didn't. So instead, he focused on her sexy smile. That turned out to be just as dangerous so he turned his attention to the amazing yacht they were on.

Yeah, he knew Munoz had bought the boat with drug money, but it was still the nicest seagoing vessel he'd ever been on. While the Navy had all kinds of cool ships from subs to aircraft carriers, they weren't the same. *Lydia's Dream* was beyond luxurious. With two pools big enough to do laps in, a sweet Jacuzzi, three bedroom suites, a temperature-controlled wine vault, and a kickass movie theater, it was almost enough to make him think he'd made a poor career choice.

Until he once again reminded himself that

Munoz had gotten rich by selling drugs and murdering people. Then it wasn't difficult remembering why he liked being a SEAL.

Nash picked up his glass. "I really wouldn't fire him. Dalton I mean. He's like a brother. And while he jokes about taking a bullet for me, the truth is, I'd take one for him, too."

Bristol regarded him curiously, like she was surprised by that. Nash cursed silently. An arms dealer like Chapman didn't risk his life for some guy who worked for him. But for some crazy reason, he wanted Bristol to know he wasn't like the other lowlife criminals her father associated with. Even if he did risk blowing his cover by doing it.

"How did you and Dalton meet?" she asked softly, slipping off her sandals and curling her legs under her. "I don't know too much about this kind of stuff, but I get the feeling you can't find a bodyguard like him on the Internet."

Nash opened his mouth then closed it again. Crap, he had no idea how to answer that. He and Dalton hadn't even considered coming up with a story to explain their connection. If he said the wrong thing, this whole mission could easily blow up in their faces.

How much did Bristol already know about

him? Her father must have told her something about Chapman, right?

He quickly fabricated a story in his head, one that was vague enough on the details to avoid any tripwires when he suddenly realized he didn't want to lie to her. It was stupid. He was working undercover for the friggin' CIA. Everything about this was a lie. He prayed Bristol wasn't involved in whatever her father had planned for those surface-to-air missiles, but for all Nash knew she could be in this stuff up to her pretty little neck. Hell, she could be playing him right now on her father's orders.

Maybe so, but he couldn't ignore the way his gut clenched when he thought about selling her on a completely made-up life. Something told him that Bristol was different, that she was nothing like her father. Nash wanted her to know the real him—or at least as much of the real him as he could tell her.

He rested his arm on the back of the seat. "We met while we were both in the Navy," he finally said, relieved he could tell her something true while still protecting his cover. Chapman had been in the Navy, so meeting Dalton there made sense. "We've watched each other's backs ever since."

Bristol did a double take. "You were in the Navy?"

He nodded.

"Huh." She studied him thoughtfully. "Is that old recruiting slogan right about it not just being a job but an adventure?"

Nash chuckled. "Oh, it's definitely an adventure."

She placed her palm on the seat and leaned forward a little, giving him a sexy glimpse of cleavage. "You can't say something like that and not expect me to want to hear more about it. What kinds of places did you get to visit? Or did you spend all your time on a ship somewhere in the middle of the ocean?"

Actually, SEALs spent very little time on a ship compared to the rest of the Navy. He couldn't tell her that though. He couldn't talk about any classified combat missions either. But there were lots of other things he could tell her about, like the places he'd been for training and mission briefings. He left out everything related to the SEALs, but at least he didn't have to lie about anything. He even told tell her a few of the tamer stories that involved Dalton, like the time his dumbass friend climbed over the wall of the Chinese Embassy in London because one of the women who worked there had smiled at him from across a crowded restaurant.

Bristol's eyes went wide. "That's insane! Did he get caught?"

He shook his head with a laugh. "No. It was close, but according to Dalton, they ended up having a very nice evening. Of course, that's only because I spent half the night running around the embassy distracting the guards so he and his new girlfriend could have a little alone time."

She smiled. "Now that's only something a real friend would do."

Nash thought back to the crazy things he and Dalton had done and was shocked to realize how many situations like that they'd been in. He wondered where this current undercover mission would rank.

"Yeah, I guess that's true," Nash admitted. "He's done the same for me. Maybe nothing as stupid since Dalton seems to have a special gift for doing boneheaded stuff that I'd never do in a million years."

"That's a relief." Bristol sipped her champagne. "I know people in the military travel a lot, but you sounded like you were away more than you were home. What kind of job did you do in the Navy?"

"I'm a SEAL."

The words were out before he realized it. He was still scrambling to say something to salvage the situation when he remembered Roman saying Chapman had been in the SEALs before getting booted out of the service. He should be good.

Then why was Bristol frowning?

"Don't you mean that you used to be a SEAL?" she asked. "You aren't in the Navy anymore."

Shit.

Damn, he really sucked at this undercover crap.

He gave her a sheepish grin. "Yeah, well, you know what they say—once a SEAL, always a SEAL. The people I worked with, the training I've had, and the things I've done will be a part of me for the rest of my life."

Her expression turned wistful. "It sounds like you really loved being in the Navy. Why did you leave it? And how did you end up going from being a SEAL to an arms dealer? That seems like a leap, not to mention goes against everything you must have believed in."

Nash hesitated. The question was innocent enough, but the way she'd asked it made him wonder if she already knew the answer. Did Munoz suspect he wasn't Chapman and was using her to find out if he was right? Considering she could barely seem to be in the same room with her father, that was unlikely. But then maybe she was a damn good actress.

Or maybe he was being overly suspicious.

He shrugged. "I'm not really sure how to answer that. One day, I'm jumping out of a plane and landing on a deck of a ship, being a hero and doing SEAL things. The next thing I know, everything has changed, the world you used to be part of is gone, and you're working with people you don't know doing things you'd never imagined doing. Sometimes it feels like you're not even yourself anymore. Like it's all make believe. Like you're playing a role without any idea what comes next."

Nash held his breath as he waited for Bristol to throw the BS flag on that esoteric pile of crap he'd just spit out, but instead she nodded.

"It's kind of like being in porn, I guess," she said lightly.

He frowned. "What?"

She laughed and waved a hand. "It's something the sports radio show host I listened to when I lived in Connecticut always said. About how nobody plans to work in porn, that they just end up there. It sounds like you didn't plan on becoming an arms dealer. You just ended up doing it."

Nash thought about it for a moment then chuckled. "I guess that's a good analogy. I sure as hell didn't plan to end up where I am, that's for sure. But I'm here now and trying my best to make sure I don't lose myself."

If Bristol thought that was a funny thing for him to say, she didn't remark on it. Instead, she gazed out at the turquoise blue water for a long time before turning her attention back to him.

"Does your family know what you do for a living?" she asked quietly.

"They have a vague idea, but I never tell them any details. They know that what I do is dangerous and we leave it at that."

That was true. His family knew he was a SEAL, that it was dangerous, and never asked a lot of questions about it. Ignorance is bliss and all that.

"Do you ever go home and see them?"

"Yeah. Not as often as I'd like though," he admitted. "With my job, getting back to Colorado can be tough."

"You're from Colorado?" she asked curiously. At least he prayed it was curiosity on her part and not the fact that she knew exactly where the real Nick Chapman was from.

He nodded. "Born and raised. I'm the middle of seven kids."

"Seven?" She gaped at him. "Seriously?"

He almost laughed. That was usually the reaction he got when he admitted he had a big family.

"Uh-huh. Three brothers and three sisters."

"Wow," she said, still clearly incredulous. "Do they all still live in Colorado?"

"Yup. My parents own an outdoor adventure company and my whole family works there. They take tourists hiking and rafting in the summer then skiing and snowmobiling in the winter."

Her lips curved. "That sounds like fun. What do they think of you not going into the family business?"

"They want me to do whatever makes me happy," he said. "I helped run the place when I was growing up and figured that I'd work there full time after graduating from high school."

"What happened?"

"I saw the ocean, that's what happened." He grinned. "My class went to California on our senior trip and I got my first look at the Pacific. Seeing those huge, rolling waves of water and seeing nothing but miles of ocean made me realize just how big the world really is."

"And you had to explore it," she murmured.

He nodded. "I joined the Navy the day I got back and left home right after I graduated. My parents weren't thrilled, but they knew it was what I wanted to do. Since I love the water and all things outdoors, becoming a SEAL was the obvious choice. I never looked back."

Bristol regarded him with something that looked like awe. "Does it make me sound horrible if I say that I'm almost jealous of you? Seeing what you want and going after it like that..." She shook her head. "I wish I could do it."

Nash was about to ask what she wanted to do and what was keeping her from it, but the captain of the ship, an older man with salt-and-pepper hair, cleared his throat to interrupt them. Crap, he'd been so caught up in Bristol that he hadn't seen the man come onto the deck.

"Forgive me for interrupting, but I just

wanted to let you know that we'll be at the island in a few minutes," he said. "After Isabella sets everything up, I'll take you ashore."

Bristol blinked. "I didn't know we were going to the island."

The captain's mouth twitched under his bushy mustache. "You know Isabella too well to think she'd let you get away with having a meal on board when there's a beautiful beach nearby. She knows how much you love the water. I'll come collect you and Señor Chapman when we're ready."

"Okay. Thanks, Alejandro."

"If you want to skip the beach, I can talk to the captain for you," Nash offered after the man left. "Tell him that we'd rather have lunch here."

She smiled. "Actually, I'd rather have lunch on the island. I was just surprised we were going there. Isabella's right. I do love the beach."

Nash loved it, too. Especially when there was a beautiful woman to share a blanket with. "What island are we going to?"

"A small private island my father owns."

Of course Munoz owned an island, Nash thought dryly. He was a cartel boss with more money than he knew what to do with. Nash wouldn't be surprised if the man owned half of

Mexico. Hopefully, that didn't include the police.

⚓

Bristol sighed as her toes sank into the warm sand. She couldn't have picked a better place to make her escape if she'd come up with it herself. The details of how she was going to get off the island were sketchy to say the least, but she'd think of something. Since the guards had stayed on the yacht instead of coming ashore with them, it should be easy enough. It was a long swim to civilization, but she was practically part dolphin when it came to the water so she was confident she could handle it. Even if she wasn't comfortable in the water, she'd still brave the ocean if it meant getting away from her father.

But first, she had to give Nick the slip.

As insane as it sounded, she felt a little badly about that. Especially since he'd risked his life to protect her from Leon last night. He'd been nothing but a gentleman since he'd arrived at the villa. That said, he was still an arms dealer who was there to do business with her father. If it came down to it, would Nick actually choose her over money?

But while the island might be the perfect place to make her getaway, being there was also a little bittersweet. She and her mother had come here a lot growing up. From playing hide and seek in between the palm trees when she was a little girl to snorkeling among the area's many colorful fish as a teenager, they were some of the happiest times of her life.

The graceful stone and terracotta gazebo just inside the beach's tree line was exactly as she remembered it. The picnic table inside was covered with a linen tablecloth and what looked like enough food to feed a small army. Bristol noticed that one of the bench seats was missing, leaving the other for her and Nick, ensuring they'd have to sit close together. No doubt Isabella was responsible for rearranging the furniture.

"You sure you're okay hanging out alone with me?" Nick asked as they stepped into the gazebo.

She set her tote on the ground and slid onto the seat. "Why wouldn't I want to be alone with you?"

He regarded her with that ridiculously charming smile of his as he sat beside her. "If I remember last night correctly, you didn't seem very keen on this outing today."

Bristol smoothed a linen napkin over her lap. "Not because of you. I hate being manipulated, and my father took it to a whole new level with that stuff he said about my mother."

She expected Nick to ask her to elaborate, but he merely nodded thoughtfully. She wasn't sure if she was relieved or not.

Still wondering about that, Bristol surveyed the table and noted that street fare tacos seemed to be the theme. In addition to Isabella's warm homemade corn tortillas waiting to be filled with spicy, perfectly-cooked pork, there were all the garnishes including guacamole, salsa, queso fresco, and cilantro, along with one of Isabella's specialties, a corn salad made with a creamy mayonnaise-based dressing laced with jalapeños, chili powder, garlic, cilantro, lime juice, and Cotija cheese.

Nick glanced at her as he added guacamole to his taco. "Can I ask you something?"

She nodded.

"While Bristol is beautiful, it doesn't strike me as a traditional Mexican name."

It wasn't exactly a question, but she didn't point that out.

"It is a little unusual I suppose." She bit into her taco and almost moaned. Isabella made the best carnitas. "My mother was born and raised in Bristol, Connecticut. She was feeling a little homesick when I was born so she named me after the town where she grew up to always remind her of it."

Understanding dawned on Nick's face. "So that's why you went up there for college."

"Yup. Mom went to Central Connecticut State University so that's where I wanted to go, too. It's only about fifteen miles from Bristol, which meant I had family nearby."

As they ate, they talked about college and her American relatives. She didn't have the crazy anecdotes Nick did, but he still laughed when she told him more fish-out-of-water stories of a sun-loving girl from Mexico floundering in the snow and freezing her butt off.

It had been a long time since she'd been able to sit and have lunch and laugh with an attractive man. It wasn't long before she found herself once again forgetting Nick was a mercenary arms dealer. He was simply a guy interested in her for the normal reasons a guy was interested in a woman.

It was beyond nice.

"What'd you go to college for?" he asked, helping himself to more corn salad.

She added a little more guacamole to her taco. "I got my bachelors in hospitality and tourism then a masters in business administration." She remembered graduation like it was yesterday. When she'd walked across the stage to get her diploma, she'd felt ready to take on the world. Little did she know what was waiting for her when she'd gotten back to Mexico. "My dream was to start my own tourism company when I came home to Manzanillo."

Nick looked up from the fresh taco he was building. "Why haven't you?"

Warning bells immediately went off in Bristol's head at the question. Nick might seem like an amazing guy, but he was still a criminal. And on her father's radar for a job. Anything she told Nick could very well end up getting back with her father. That wouldn't be good, even if her father already knew what she thought of him.

But despite all that she had an overwhelming need to tell Nick everything, to hell with the risk.

"My father wouldn't allow it because that would mean letting me leave the compound, and that won't be happening."

Nick regarded her in silence for a long time. Bristol's stomach clenched. Crap. Had she made a mistake saying anything?

"Are you telling me that you're a prisoner in your own home?" he finally asked.

Bristol hesitated. If she answered his question honestly, there would be no going back.

"Yes," she admitted quietly. "This is the first time I've been allowed off the property since my father murdered my mother."

"*Murdered* her?" Something told Bristol that very little caught Nick off guard, but he looked genuinely stunned right then. He set his uneaten taco on the colorful plate in front of him and turned to face her, swinging one leg over the bench so he was straddling it. "Tell me everything."

She considered giving him the abridged version, but then changed her mind. "I knew there was something wrong the day I got back from college. My parents had a welcome-home party for me, but the tension was so thick between them that I could barely breathe. I only found out later from Isabella that it was because my mother had just discovered my father was a major player in the Amador cartel."

Nick frowned. "How was it possible for your mother not to know?"

She moved the small pile of corn salad around with her fork on her plate, not looking at him. "Believe me, I've been asking myself the same question a dozen times a day over the past year. Maybe love really is blind."

When Nick didn't say anything, she sighed. Setting her fork down, she shifted on the seat, sitting cross-legged on the bench so she could look at him.

"Regardless, they had a huge fight. My father told my mother he'd get out of the cartel and we'd all move somewhere far away from here. It was a lie, of course. He never had any intention of leaving."

"So, he killed her," Nick said.

"Yes. But not because she pushed him to leave the cartel."

Bristol told Nick about Leon kissing her and how he'd punched her after she rebuffed him. Nick's face darkened with anger, but he didn't interrupt. When she got to the part about her mother disappearing, tears filled her eyes.

"What happened?" Nick prompted as her

voice trailed off.

"She never came back," Bristol whispered, remembering how frantic she'd been. She'd sat in her room beside her packed suitcase for hours, thinking the worst. But even she hadn't imagined something so heinous.

She was so caught up in those painful memories she barely realized Nick had taken her hands in his. It felt good...and somehow made it easier to tell the rest of the story.

"I know in my heart that my father ordered Leon to kill my mother. For no other reason than because she was going to leave him...and take me with her. Not because he loves us, but because he isn't the kind of man who lets anyone walk away from him."

Nick rubbed his thumb along the back of her hand. "I know it's a lame thing to say and won't do anything to make you feel better, but I'm truly sorry about your mother."

She nodded. "Thank you."

"What did you do after you found out about your mother?" he asked.

"I tried to leave, but without money and my US passport I couldn't get on a plane or even across the border. Leon tracked down the bus I was on anyway. He dragged me home and threatened to beat me to death if I ever tried it again. Not that it mattered because my father's guards didn't let me out of their sight for months."

It was only recently that they'd stopped following her around inside the villa. Unfortunately, they still patrolled the property.

Nick muttered something under his breath she didn't catch. "What about the police?"

"I called them and found out that my father owns this city, or at least the cops in it."

"Of course he does," Nick said. "What happened?"

"Not much," she admitted. "Two detectives showed up at the villa and told my father everything I'd said. Then they laughed and told him that he needed to keep me under control. They treated my mother's death like a joke. Since I have dual citizenship, I thought about calling my family in Connecticut and asking them to get the American embassy involved, but after the cops left my father made sure I didn't have access to a phone or a computer."

"What about Isabella? Surely she would have called for you."

Bristol gave him a sad smile. "I know she

would have. But I'm afraid of what my father would do to her if she did."

Nick scowled but didn't say anything, and she wished she could figure out what he was thinking. But his dark eyes betrayed nothing.

She still wasn't sure why she'd opened up to Nick. Or what he might do with the information she'd just given him. She had an overwhelming urge to trust him, but what if he did what the police had done and went straight to her father with everything she'd told him?

Would it really matter if he did? With any luck she'd be far away from here by tonight. If she couldn't get to the American embassy then she'd pay a coyote to smuggle her across the border.

"What if I said I could help you?" Nick asked suddenly.

Her breath caught, but she refused to let herself hope. "What do you mean?"

Nick glanced out at the yacht anchored off the beach before turning back to her, his dark eyes searching hers, mesmerizing and calculating at the same time. "I can't go into details, but I promise I'm going to make sure your father pays for what he did to your mother. Then I'm going to kick Leon's ass for what he did to you." He brushed her windswept hair back from her face. "You're never going to be anyone's prisoner ever again, you have my word on that."

Bristol's heart beat a little faster. Against all expectations, she found herself believing for the first time in a year that there might truly be a way out of this nightmare. But then a little voice of doubt began murmuring in the back of her mind, telling her this was too good to be true.

"Why would you go against a man like my father and risk everything for a woman you met two days ago?"

He cupped her face gently in his hand. "Because something tells me you're worth the risk. Even if that means going up against a man like your father."

The words were plain and straightforward, but she was starting to get the feeling that plain and straightforward pretty much described Nick Chapman. And she believed every word he said.

She abruptly remembered her tote beside them. When she'd left the villa a few hours ago she'd been ready to do whatever it took to be free of her father, including swimming all the way to the United States if she had to. But Nick had given her another option.

She opened her mouth the thank him, but then decided to show him how grateful she was instead.

When their lips came together, she felt a little tingle zip through her unlike anything she'd ever experienced. Then Nick buried his fingers in her hair and tugged her close, making several other parts of her body hum. His tongue teased its way into her mouth and she let out a little sound of pleasure at how good he tasted. Or maybe he was the one who moaned. She wasn't quite sure.

Bristol had kissed guys in high school and college. She'd even had a steady boyfriend her junior year up in Connecticut. But as she plunged her tongue deeper into Nick's mouth, tangling, teasing, and tasting, she realized she hadn't ever been kissed like this.

She didn't know when her hands had climbed up his broad shoulders and locked behind his strong neck, keeping him exactly where she wanted him. But they were there now and they knew exactly what they were doing. Nick's free hand glided along her bare thigh, sliding underneath the cover-up she wore to settle on her hip. Heat pooled between her legs, and she suddenly wanted to do far more than simply kiss him. She wanted to make love to him right there in the gazebo.

She trailed one hand down his chest and over his rock-hard abs with every intention of heading further south when Nick pulled away with a groan. She started to tug him in for another kiss when the ocean breeze carried laughter from the yacht in their direction.

She stiffened.

Crap. There was a whole boat full of her father's guards watching her and Nick. How could she have forgotten that?

Nick cursed under his breath, glancing at the yacht. "I wondered why your father sent so many guards with us. Now I realize it was so they could spy for him. No doubt he'll think this means I'm leaning toward taking that job he's offering me." He turned to look at her again, his dark eyes intense. "Your father would be right. But only so I can take him down."

CHAPTER
Six

WHEN I SUGGESTED YOU SHOULD FIND A GIRLFRIEND, I didn't mean the daughter of the drug cartel boss we're trying to send to prison," Dalton murmured as Nash opened up another box of ammunition and dug through it.

Nash glanced at Munoz and his men standing behind the firing line of the cartel boss's personal gun range to make sure they hadn't heard what Dalton said. But they were a few hundred feet away and much more interested in the new Russian automatic weapons they were going to get to play with. The jackasses were acting like it was Christmas in July.

The range complex was a few miles from the main compound, and though it was large enough to fire almost any weapon anyone might want as well as house several bunkers to store all those weapons and their ammunition—as well as explosives—it wasn't very secure. All it had was a simple gate with one guard.

Nash slipped a handful of short, round, fragmentation cartridges into the pockets of his tactical vest. "It's a little late to point that out since I'm already in a committed relationship with Bristol."

Dalton gaped at him. "Committed relationship. Are you mental? You just met two days ago. People don't fall in love in two days. At least not outside a romance book with heaving bosoms and Scottish men in kilts on the covers."

Nash stared at his best friend, not sure if he really wanted to know how the hell Dalton knew what they did in romance books. On second thought, he didn't want to know.

"I'm joking," he said.

Dalton lifted a brow as if to say he didn't quite believe that.

Nash sighed. "Look, I'm just trying to help Bristol. Munoz already murdered her mother. He wouldn't hesitate to do the same to her."

His friend gave him an appraising look. "So, that's what the kiss on the beach was about, you trying to help Bristol. Funny, because it sure looked like you were enjoying it to me."

Nash couldn't stop the grin tugging at the corner of his mouth as he remembered the kiss he and Bristol had shared yesterday. Simply put, it had been amazing.

"I knew it," Dalton muttered. "You do have a thing for her."

Nash grabbed another box of ammunition. Munoz had enough of the stuff to outfit a small army. Or start World War III.

"Okay, maybe I do," Nash admitted. "Bristol is a very beautiful woman."

"And what?" Dalton asked scornfully. "You think this thing between you and her is going to turn into something? That Bristol is going to jump into your bed when she discovers you're not Nick Chapman, that you don't really live in Europe, and that everything else you've told her is a lie?"

Nash scowled. "I don't know and to tell the truth, I haven't thought that far. I'm doing what seems right at the moment and seeing where it leads me.

Shaking his head, Dalton reached in the open ammo box and pulled out a few more of the 40mm grenades for the weapons demonstration Nash was about to put on for Munoz's men. "You really like her, don't you? You're hoping this thing with her works out."

There was no point in lying. "Yeah, I guess so. That said, I can't see this ending well, no matter how much I like Bristol."

"That's too bad," Dalton said. "Since she's probably the only woman who's ever going to kiss you without you paying them"

Nash flipped his friend the bird. "Enough about me and my so-called committed relationship. What have you been up to since yesterday? Roman and I stopped by your room last night but you weren't there."

Dalton fell into step beside him as he turned and headed toward the group of men waiting for the demonstration to start. "I went into town with some of the guards."

Nash did a double take. "You're getting all buddy-buddy with them now?"

His friend shrugged. "We all understand what it's like working for rich jackasses who don't appreciate us. We spent hours yesterday talking trash about you and Munoz while you were eating lunch on the beach and making out with the boss's daughter. You get a few drinks into these guys and it's amazing what kind of shit they'll slip up and tell you."

Nash stopped walking to look at Dalton. He wanted to ask what kind of crap his friend had said about him to Munoz's men because a few of them were looking at him funny this morning, but that would have to wait until later. Right now, he was more interested in what Munoz's goons had to say. "Like what?"

"Well, for one thing, all of his guys are pretty sure Munoz is preparing to make a major move up the cartel food chain. He might have money falling out his wazoo, but it turns out he's rather low down the ladder when it comes to real power in the organization. The other Amador bosses humor him because he controls the shipping fleets that move their drugs in and out of this part of the world, but they don't pay any attention when he makes suggestions about how they could improve their business model or branch out into other criminal activities."

Nash chuckled. "That must frost his nads."

"Which is why he's going to do something about it. He's been stockpiling weapons for nearly a year now, as well as making deals with the local cops, the Federales, and the Mexican Army. His men think he's going to war with several of the bosses. Maybe all the way up to Amador."

Damn. Nash couldn't imagine trying to make a move that aggressive against a crime syndicate as spread out as the Amador cartel. There was no way they wouldn't see it coming.

"Have you told Roman or the other guys about this?"

Dalton shook his head. "Nah. I don't trust those guys as far as I can throw them. Let them figure it out on their own. They're supposed to be the spies here, not us."

Nash couldn't necessarily disagree with that. Since they'd gotten here, Roman, Shaw, and Santiago hadn't done much of anything but sit around with Munoz and drink beer. If they were close to figuring out what Munoz was up to, or who the Russian arms dealer was, they'd never mentioned it to him and Dalton.

He began heading toward the firing line, then stopped to face Dalton again. "You said you were talking trash about me with the other guards. Is that why so many of them are looking at me sideways this morning?"

"Probably."

Nash resisted the urge to punch his friend.

"So, what exactly did you say?"

Dalton shrugged like it wasn't a big deal, but the grin on his face gave him away. "I might have mentioned that you're hoping to marry your way into the cartel since there's no chance of you getting there purely on your own abilities. I made sure everyone knew it's not your fault you're lacking a little testosterone since you lost your balls in a freak farming accident a few years ago and all."

Nash shook his head. Well, that explained the strange looks he'd gotten all morning.

He turned to make his way toward Munoz and the other men when Dalton put a hand on his shoulder, stopping him. "All joking aside, I did learn one important thing while I was hanging out with Munoz's guards that you need to know."

"What's that?"

Dalton motioned with his chin toward where Munoz stood talking with Leon. "That you need to watch out for Leon. The guy has been a head case since Munoz found him in Columbia and brought him back here. In the words of the guys I talked to, Leon is a serial killer who enjoys watching people die. Not only that, but he's also insanely loyal to Munoz. If he thinks you're bad for his boss—or that you're trying to come between them—he'll gut you in a second."

"I'll keep that in mind," Nash said and started walking again.

The 40mm grenade lofted toward the target—a beat-up taxi cab about 350 meters from the firing line—and impacted the ground near the driver's side door. The boom of the high-explosive cartridge going off wasn't that bad from this distance, but the blast blew out every window in the vehicle, and the BB-sized fragments turned the side of the car into swiss cheese.

Nash lowered the combined assault rifle-grenade launcher, slowly turning to take in the collection of men in front of him. He'd just put five grenades within a foot of their intended target, destroying all of them in the span of about thirty seconds. That seemed to make his audience pay attention, which was something.

When he and Dalton had gotten to the range earlier, Nash assumed he'd be showing Munoz and his men how to set up and use the high-tech Russian surface-to air missiles the cartel boss had purchased, but it turned out that Roman hadn't given him the missiles yet. Probably because he didn't have them yet. That was a good thing as far as Nash was concerned. The longer Roman was able to keep those missiles out of Munoz's hands, the better.

So, he'd spent the past hour going over the finer points of using the AK-74. That had turned out to be a waste of time for the most part since Munoz's men were of the opinion that they already knew how to shoot an automatic weapon. Based on the live fire session they'd just finished though, while the cartel guys were definitely good at squeezing the trigger and sending a lot of metal downrange, they couldn't hit the broad side of a barn.

On the bright side, at least he didn't have to feel like he was making the world a more dangerous place with these demonstrations since these guys were too stupid to learn anything he was teaching.

He was just getting into the detailed instructions on how to load the grenade in the muzzle of the launcher and adjust the sights on the right side of the weapon when a loud laugh from Leon interrupted him. Nash ground his jaw. The asshole had made snide comments in Spanish the entire morning, insisting nothing Nash showed them was all that difficult.

"You want to come up and show us how it's done, Leon?" Nash asked, holding the weapon out.

Leon shook his head.

"What?" Nash demanded. "You aren't intimidated by a little grenade launcher are you?"

The dare had the desired effect. Munoz and the rest of his men regarded Leon expectantly, clearly waiting to see if he was going to take that burn lying down. He didn't. Cursing in Spanish, he strode over to Nash and grabbed the weapon from his hand.

It quickly became obvious that Leon hadn't been paying attention to the demonstration. It took him forever to load the grenade into the muzzle and even longer to adjust the sights.

"Need a little help?" Nash jabbed.

Leon muttered something in Spanish but otherwise ignored him. Pressing the butt end of the grenade launcher against his shoulder, Leon lined up the weapon and pulled the trigger. The grenade hit the ground and exploded on impact thirty feet from the target. If Leon had been aiming at the same target Nash hit a few moments earlier, which wasn't a given.

"Looks like you're a little short," Nash said. "I bet you hear that a lot though."

Leon rounded on him, dark eyes filled with hatred. "Weapons like this are for cowards!" Tossing the grenade launcher on the ground, Leon reached behind his back and came out with a wicked looking knife. "A real man has the courage to get up close to the person he intends to kill and look him in the eyes as he slides his blade between his ribs and guts him like a fish."

"Unless the other man takes the knife away and beats the shit out of you." Nash moved a little away from the row of tables along the firing line. He wanted space to work if Leon decided to mix it up. "It's a lot harder to look like a tough guy when you're trying to pull your own blade out of your ass."

Leon glared at him, his hand tightening around the hilt of the weapon.

Out of the corner of his eye, Nash caught a glimpse of Munoz standing off to the side, his arms crossed over his chest as he watched the show along with everyone else.

Nash turned is attention back to Leon just as the man took a swing at him with the blade. Nash had to leap backward to avoid getting his stomach slashed open. He guessed the a-hole really did want to gut him like a fish.

"I'm going to enjoy hearing you beg for mercy," Leon said.

Nash snorted. "From what I hear, you only get off on hurting women. It's a whole different ball game when you fuck with someone your own size."

Letting out an expletive, Leon lowered his head and charged Nash like a bull. The moment he got close, Nash grabbed him by the front of the shirt, slamming his knee into Leon's gut then hitting the ground in a backward roll, taking his opponent with him.

Leon sailed over Nash's head, coming down hard on his back, air exploding from his lungs. Nash jumped to his feet, wanting to be ready in case Leon came at him again. Sure enough, the bastard lunged for him, swinging that big-ass knife and almost slicing open Nash's throat this time. Nash jerked out of the way just in time then blocked the backhand slash that followed. But the defensive move only earned him a solid punch to the jaw that sent him staggering back and seeing double for a second.

Nash backed away fast giving himself a moment to recover. He'd underestimated Leon. The guy might not be a trained martial arts fighter, but he was a street brawler, and that made him just as dangerous.

Leon darted forward, going to Nash's thigh. Nash deflected the strike then planted his hand on Leon's chest and shoved hard. Nash followed up with a series of right hooks that sent Leon stumbling back, blood coming from his nose and the gash over his left eye.

Nash was vaguely aware of the other men shouting and cheering around them. But it wasn't until he heard Dalton saying he'd cover someone's two-thousand peso bet that he realized the crowd was wagering on the outcome of the fight.

At least Dalton was betting on him to win.

Leon tried to carve Nash with the knife again, mixing in rapid slashes with sharp jabs. The man was damn fast for his size, and while Nash got in a few punches, he spent more time trying to keep the blade away from anything vital. That earned him a few cuts on the forearms, biceps, and ribs.

"Stop screwing around and do something," Dalton shouted from the sideline. "I have a hundred-thousand pesos riding on you."

Nash ignored his friend as he blocked the knife for what seemed like the hundredth time.

"I'm going to enjoy telling Bristol all about how I killed you today," Leon said softly. Maybe so Munoz wouldn't hear. "I wonder if she'll cry when she hears you're dead. If not, she will after I'm done with her."

Anger surged through Nash. He didn't need Leon to spell it out to know what he had in mind for Bristol.

He really hated this piece of shit.

Jaw tight, Nash forced himself to wait until Leon charged him yet again. When he did, Nash brought his fist down on the back of Leon's knife hand, sending the blade skittering across the ground. Before Leon could react, Nash punched him hard in the throat.

The jackass stumbled back choking and coughing. He wasn't so tough now that he didn't have his precious knife.

Nash delivered a kick to Leon's balls that doubled him over, then followed that with another kick to the inside of the man's left knee. Leon would have gone down for sure, but Nash grabbed a handful of Leon's hair, holding him up and punching him over and over in the face, backing him across the range as the men watching quickly moved out of the way. By the time Nash let him go, Leon crumpled to the ground, bleeding and semi-conscious.

Sunlight glinted off something near his foot and Nash glanced down to see Leon's knife lying in the dirt. Before he even realized what he was doing, Nash snatched up the knife and moved toward Leon.

Dalton was at his side in a flash, his hand on Nash's arm. "It's over, bro. Fight's done."

Nash rounded on his friend, ready to rip Dalton a new one. But then he saw the concern on Dalton's face and knew his buddy was right. He couldn't kill Leon, no matter how much he wanted to.

He glanced Munoz's way and found the man regarding him with a thoughtful expression. What the hell was going on in the cartel boss's head?

"You cool?" Dalton asked.

Nash nodded. "I'm good."

"Great." Dalton smacked him on the shoulder hard enough for it to sting. "Then you won't mind if I go collect my winnings."

CHAPTER
Seven

BRISTOL WAS SURPRISED WHEN SHE WALKED INTO THE kitchen and found Nick digging around in the big freezer. She thought he'd be out all day doing some kind of weapons demonstration. They must have finished early. For some reason, that fact made her ridiculously happy. Something she hadn't been in a long time. And she owed it all to an illegal arms dealer, a man for all accounts and purposes she should be terrified of.

But Nick was different than the usual run-of-the-mill criminal who frequented the villa. He'd demonstrated that on the beach yesterday.

"Need any help finding whatever you're looking for in there?" she asked.

He turned, ice cubes piled high in the towel he held. His arms and shoulders were smeared with what could only be blood. More seeped from the cut on his temple, running down the side of his face.

"What happened?" she demanded.

Heart suddenly hammering like crazy, she closed the distance between them at a run even though she didn't have a clue what to do for the wound. Should she call for help or try doing first-aid herself?

Nick set the towel down on the counter then gently put a big hand on each of her shoulders with a sexy smile that made her pulse race for an entirely different reason. She gave her self a mental shake. He was bleeding. How could she be thinking about how good looking he was at a moment like this?

Maybe because he was so damn attractive that a little blood just made him look hotter?

"Calm down," he said. "It's not as bad as it looks."

She took in the myriad cuts covering his forearms and biceps then the bruise starting to form along his jaw. "It looks pretty bad to me."

"Not really. I've cut myself worse shaving. After I clean up, you'll barely notice it."

Bristol seriously doubted that. Reaching out, she ran a finger lightly over one of the closed-up cuts on his arm. It wasn't very deep, but it was straight and surgical, like someone had sliced him with a razor blade.

Or a knife.

She only knew one person who carried a knife.

"Leon did this, didn't he?" she demanded.

Anger welled up inside her, followed quickly by fear. Leon had attacked Nick because word had gotten back to him about the kiss they'd shared on the beach. The realization that she was this worried about a man she'd just met and had only kissed once was as scary as his injuries.

Nick shook his head. "Nah. I went jogging this morning around the compound and got attacked by some kind of strange creature. I'm pretty sure it was a Chupacabra."

"Uh-huh." How could he be so cavalier about something so serious? "Forget about that for now. Isabella keeps some first-aid supplies in the bathroom the serving staff uses. You can tell me what happened while I fix you up."

Nick didn't say anything as she took his hand and led him out the side door of the kitchen and down a short hallway to the part of the house where Isabella and the rest of the serving staff lived.

By the time they got to the bathroom, Bristol's pulse was back to something resembling normal. Nick leaned back against the counter as she opened the door of the linen closet and its shelves upon shelves of first-aid supplies. Isabella said they were there for when the landscapers cut themselves, but Bristol wasn't naive. The boxes of bandages, rubber gloves, antiseptic and antibiotic ointments, trauma kits, and minor surgical equipment wasn't merely for the groundskeepers. They were for her father's guards. The men who worked for him had a habit of getting severely wounded in his employment.

Bristol wasn't as good with this kind of stuff as Isabella, but she'd taken a first-aid class in college. Even if she hadn't, she wouldn't let anyone else take care of Nick. He'd gotten hurt because of her. The least she could do was tend to his wounds.

"Take off your shirt," Bristol said over her shoulder as she grabbed a bottle of antiseptic wash along with gauze, bandages, and tape. "This is supposed to be non-irritating. But it's probably still going to sting."

"Don't worry about it," Nick said.

She turned to dump the armload of stuff

onto the bathroom vanity counter and found Nick
still leaning back against the counter without his
shirt.

Bristol tried not to stare...and failed. It wasn't
her fault. In her experience, men simply didn't
have bodies like Nick's. Every muscle of his abs,
obliques, pecs, and shoulders was defined and
sculpted like a work of art. If he wasn't bleeding
she would have taken the opportunity to ogle him
for a while.

Bristol's hands shook a little as she opened
the box of gauze and squirted a healthy amount of
the antiseptic wash on one of the pads. She took a
deep breath before, forcing herself to focus.

That proved difficult with Nick looking so
damn perfect. She found it hard to know where to
look—at his smiling face that was so handsome it
was hard to even breathe when she did, or at his
chest that made her want to run her hands all over
it just to see if those muscles felt as good as she
suspected.

It was the blood on his arms that finally
brought her back to reality. Nick might be amazing, mouth watering, and mesmerizing, but he
was hurt, and that tore out her heart.

She started on his left forearm, gently wiping

away the dried blood crusted over the nearly par-allel slices running from wrist to elbow. There were others higher up on the outside of the biceps and a few across the left side of his ribcage, but she ignored those for now. One perfect part at a time, she told herself.

"What happened?" she asked, flinching a little when fresh blood started to flow from the wounds. Part of her wanted to stop, worried she was making it worse, but she knew they had to be cleaned.

"Leon was being an asshole during the weap-ons demonstration," Nick said, apparently not affected at all by what she was doing. It wasn't that he was being stoic. It was more like he sim-ply didn't seem to notice the pain she had to be in-flicting. "Maybe he heard about us kissing on the beach. Regardless, he kept pushing me, trying to provoke a reaction and looking for a fight. I got tired of his crap and finally decided to accommo-date him."

She finished with his forearm, adding a thick antibiotic gel to help stop the fresh bleeding and wrapping a bandage around the entire area. Then she moved to his left bicep. The cuts there weren't as deep, but she found herself spending more time on them simply because she enjoyed touching him.

"I'm assuming Leon had a knife?" she asked even though it was obvious.

"Yeah." Nick snorted. "It might just be me but I think he's compensating for something."

"Did you have a knife, too?"

Nick shook his head. "Nah. I wanted Leon to feel like he had a chance."

She frowned at him. "Are you ever serious about anything?"

Nick grabbed the hand she'd been cleaning him with and tugged her so close her tank-top covered breasts were touching his muscled chest. "There is one thing I'm very serious about," he whispered in a warm whisper, the low rumble of his voice making goosebumps rise up all over her body. "Maybe we should put the first-aid on hold for now so we can talk about it."

The goosebumps immediately turned into tingles as his mouth came perilously close to hers. She desperately wanted to kiss him again, but she knew if she went down that path she wouldn't get back to cleaning him up until who knew when.

She reluctantly took a step back, carefully disengaging her hand from his and going back to cleaning a shallow cut across the top of his bicep.

"You should take Leon seriously," she admonished. "He could have killed you."

Nick didn't say anything for a time. "Maybe. Or I could have killed him. I was prepared to for what he did to you and your mother."

Bristol met Nick's gaze, wondering if he was finally being serious. The intensity in his dark eyes told her that he was. He would have killed Leon...for her. She wasn't quite sure how to take that.

They both fell silent as she cleaned the rest of the cuts on his arms, then did the same to the ones on his ribs before finally moving up to his face. The act of carefully moving her fingers over his warm skin was almost hypnotizing. That was when she noticed they were breathing in time together. What they were doing was as transcendent for him as it was for her.

By the time she finished wiping the blood from his scruff and applying antibiotic cream to the crease above his left brow to keep it from bleeding, Bristol knew in her heart there was something insanely special going on between them. Yesterday, she'd hoped he might be able to help her out of the horrible situation she was in. Now, all she could think about was where this thing with Nick would go next.

Without a word, he slipped one hand into her long, dark hair, tugging her close and kissing her so hard it made her breathless. She wrapped an arm around his neck, pulling him in. He parted his lips and she took the invitation to dip her tongue in, reveling in the taste as she felt his free hand slip down to slide over her butt. He squeezed her ass, pulling her more tightly against him until she could feel every part of that perfect body of his. His cock stiffened in his dusty uniform pants, and she ground against him, empowered at knowing she was making him this excited simply with a kiss.

She moaned against his mouth as he cupped her ass with his other hand, too, almost yanking her off her toes as he fitted her against him more snuggly and moving his hips in a way that told her exactly how much he wanted her at that moment. Her body began to hum, and she was almost embarrassed by how turned on she was. At this rate she might orgasm before they got their clothes off.

Bristol yearned to slide her hand down his chest and over his abs to caress his hard-on through his pants, but he was pressed up against her too tightly for that. Instead, she made do with wrapping her arm around him and caressing his well-sculpted back.

Nick did some exploring of his own, and her breath caught as he slid one hand up and over her hip, slipping teasing fingers under the hem of her shirt, tracing them lightly across the bare skin of her side, moving higher. She murmured her approval against his mouth, encouraging him to shove her shirt all the way up, tear off her bra and run his hungry mouth over every bare inch of her tingling body.

The urge was so overwhelming, she was ready to make love right there on the vanity counter...or even up against the wall.

She was about to start begging when Nick suddenly pulled away and urged her back, putting some space between them. She opened her mouth to ask him what was wrong, but the words died on her lips at the sound of heavy footsteps in the hallway. A split second later, her father stepped into the open doorway of the bathroom.

"There you are, Nick." Her father's gaze slid over them, then the gauze, bandages and antiseptic bottle still on the counter. "I see Bristol tended to your injuries."

"I was more than ready to rub some dirt on

them and call it good, but your daughter suggested first aid," Nick said smoothly.

Her father gave her an approving look. "Bristol can be practical once she recognizes something is in her best interest. She got that from her mother."

Fury filled Bristol like it did every time he mentioned her mother, and she stepped forward. Nick caught her arm before she could do anything. Not that she was sure what she would have done. Punching her father would have been satisfying though.

Her father didn't seem to notice her anger. Or maybe he simply didn't care.

"After you get cleaned up, come to my study," he said to Nick. "There's something I'd like to discuss with you."

Without waiting for a reply, he turned and walked out, leaving her alone with her anger...and Nick.

Bristol turned and began cleaning up. Before she'd done more than stuff a few gauze pads back into their box, Nick was behind her, his body pressed up against hers, his arms around her waist. It was impossible to miss the way his still hard erection nestled up against her bottom.

"Don't believe for a second I'm not thinking

about finishing what we started," he said softly in her ear.

Then Nick was gone, his booted footsteps echoing along the hall.

As she slowly finished cleaning up, she couldn't help smiling as she imagined what it might be like if they ever did get the chance to finish what they'd started.

⚓

"You don't seem the worst for wear," Munoz remarked.

Nash took the glass of expensive single malt the man offered and dropped into the leather wing chair positioned in front of the cartel boss's desk. It had taken him a few minutes to change clothes, but after a quick conversation with Dalton, he'd come straight to Munoz's study as requested.

He leaned back in his seat, his gaze drawn to the painting of a beautiful dark-haired woman on the wall behind the desk. For half a second, he thought the portrait was of Bristol, but the woman's skin was much lighter, and he realized it must be Bristol's mother. Nash couldn't believe the cartel boss kept her picture in his study after he'd had her killed. Then again, maybe Munoz kept it as some kind of weird trophy. Or a constant reminder to Bristol.

The thought made Nash want to kill the cartel boss.

"Considering the fact that you were unarmed and Leon had a knife, one might say you came out of the fight nearly unscathed," Munoz added as he moved around behind the desk and sat down.

Picking up a polished wooden box, Munoz took off the lid and held it out. Nash could smell the sweet aroma of tobacco from where he sat. He shook his head, declining the offer.

"I got a few scratches, nothing more," Nash said in reply to Munoz comment. "I'm sure you didn't ask me to come here to talk about my cuts and bruises. Why don't we get to the point and talk about the fight Leon and I got into instead. I get the feeling it was supposed to be some kind of test."

Munoz clipped the end off a cigar, then lit it slowly and carefully, eyeing him the whole time. "It was. I needed to know what kind of man you really are when pushed."

Nash almost laughed. This clown had no idea what kind of man he was when pushed. But he was going to find out before this mission was over. "Why do you care what kind of man I am since it seems that neither you nor the men who work for you are interested in the training you're paying me to provide?"

Munoz puffed on his cigar and relaxed back in his pricey leather chair. "You're right. I'm not interested in the weapons training you're here to give. I'm interested in your other talents."

Nash sipped his whiskey, but didn't say anything. He loved the sweet undertones you got with Scotch Whiskey. It was the only kind of alcohol he ever wasted his time on.

"What do you think of my daughter?" Munoz asked.

Nash's hand tightened around the glass. How the hell was he supposed to answer that? It wasn't like he could admit he still tasted Bristol on his lips from the make-out session they'd had earlier. No more than he could say that pulling away from her when he'd heard Munoz coming down the hallway had been one of the hardest things he'd ever done in his life.

Bristol had looked so damn edible right then,

her eyes glazed with lust, her lips plump and inviting, her hands clutching at his shoulders as she'd tried to keep him from pushing her away. There was no doubt in his mind that if they hadn't been interrupted they'd still be going at it right now. With absolutely no friggin' clothes on.

No, he most definitely couldn't tell that to Munoz.

"She's an amazing woman," he finally said.

Munoz breathed out a thick cloud of smoke through his nose then pointed his cigar at Nash. "You're not a braggart. I can see why Bristol likes you. And she does like you. A father knows these things. But just as importantly, she respects you as well. You two would make a good couple."

Before Nash could point out that maybe Bristol would like to decide that for herself, Munoz reached under his desk and came out with a large metal briefcase, thumping it down on the desk.

"Have you ever thought of working full time for someone instead of all this freelance work you do?" Munoz asked, slowly flicking the numbered dial on the front of the case before popping the latches. He spun it around to face Nash without opening the lid. "And before you answer, Edein

Gojkic already told me that if I wanted to recruit you, I would need to start with a large sum of money and an attractive woman. You've already met the woman. Now meet the large sum of money."

Munoz flipped open the briefcase, displaying stacks of neatly bundled American hundred-dollar bills, complete with those little colored paper cuffs around them like they had in banks. Just for the fun of it, Nash did the math in his head, figuring there had to be at least $500,000 in front of him. That was more money in one place than he'd ever seen in his life. Not that he would even know what to do with that kind of money if he had it, but he had to admit, it was fun looking at it.

"This is just the signing bonus," Munoz added. "If you come to work for me, you'll get another briefcase like this every other month like clockwork."

As if to add emphasis, Munoz flipped one of the stacks in his direction. Nash caught it without thinking, wondering where a cartel boss got crisp bank-wrapped bills like this. But then the significance of the cartel boss's earlier words filtered through. Munoz had just given him one of the pieces of information they'd been looking for.

"So, Edein voluntarily gave you tips on what it would take to steal me away from him? I'm surprised," Nash said casually.

He had no idea who the hell Edein Gojkic was, but something told him the man had to be Nick Chapman's current employer, the Russian arms dealer.

Munoz laughed. "It's the Russian in his blood that makes him pragmatic. He knows if you end up working for me, it likely means more arms deals for him. He would consider that a win-win situation. Though I have to admit, I don't think he honestly thought I could lure you away. Of course, he's never met my daughter."

Nash was torn between being thrilled and pissed. He was thrilled he now had the name of the Russian arms dealer they were after. But at the same time, the casual way Munoz was ready to use his daughter as a perk if Nash worked for him was just plain shitty.

If the rest of this mission worked out right, Bristol wouldn't have to deal with her asshole father much longer. Until then, Nash was going to have to suck up his disdain.

"I have a few simple questions before I decide if I want to work for you," he said, flipping the stack of $10,000 back into the briefcase.

Munoz nodded, puffing his cigar.

"What are you going to do with Leon?" he said bluntly. "Not that I give a shit really, but you have to realize there will be trouble between us if I decide to stay."

"Leon has served his purpose," Munoz said. "He has been a loyal soldier and useful to have around, but he has always been limited in his contributions to the organization and will never go further than his brawn and ruthlessness will let him. His job can be filled by another easily enough."

Shit, talk about cold-blooded. Even for a drug cartel boss.

"And what would I be doing if I decided to work for you?"

Munoz leaned forward eagerly. "The cartels in Mexico—Amador included—are dying. It's a slow death by a thousand-and-one paper cuts as the Federales and the army continue to take out members of our senior leadership one man at a time. Others move up to take their places of course, but each time this happens, the organization is weakened, and the next man up becomes more and more fixated on collecting wealth in the fastest way possible without regard to a long-term plan, much less the future at all."

"You have a different vision for the cartels?"

Munoz nodded. "First and foremost, we need to move our focus away from North America. Eastern Europe, Russia, China, India...that's where we've seen future growth in our business. At the same time, we need to branch out and diversify into other profitable activities. Illegal arms to be sure, but also industrial hacking and other cyber crimes at the global level. Of course, all of these new ventures require someone familiar with the international crime world. That's where you come in. With my money and vision, and your connections, we could take the cartel in a completely new direction. We'd both be rich beyond belief."

Nash had to admit he was surprised. This wasn't where he'd expected this conversation to go. Selling drugs in other parts of the world? Yeah, that he could believe. But industrial hacking and cyber crimes? That was next level stuff for a criminal organization. More like what you'd expect from a rogue nation like North Korea or Russia.

Munoz actually *did* have vision. But that vision didn't explain one very critical detail. A detail

Roman and the CIA were keen on figuring out.

"That sounds impressive, but what does any of this have to do with the missiles you purchased?" Nash asked. "How do they fit into your new cartel vision?"

Munoz shrugged. "There are few in positions of authority within the organization that would accept that vision. Therefore, they need to be eliminated."

"You're going to use the missiles to take out the other Amador bosses?" Nash asked. "I'm not sure I see how that's going to work. What are you going to do, shoot them out of the air when they're heading out on vacation?"

"I won't be going after the cartel bosses themselves. That would be a waste of time. If I cut off one of the snake's heads, another would simply grow to replace it. I want you to take out a military aircraft carrying a general by the name of Carlos Medina Mora."

Nash was curious despite himself. "Okay. What will taking out a general do for you? And that would take one missile. What about the other four missiles you've bought? How are you going to use those?"

"Targeting General Mora makes sense if you

understand that he's the man who runs the anti-cartel task force and works directly with the Attorney General's office. He's a hero to the people of Mexico, boldly leading attacks against not just the Amador cartel, but also others. Most would be terribly disappointed to know that General Mora is also corrupt and takes money from the very criminals he professes to hate so much."

"Corruption in the government? Say it isn't so," Nash quipped. "But if he's already on the cartel payroll, why take him out?"

"Because if he's killed by someone in the cartels, the public outcry for retribution will be impossible to ignore. Those responsible for his death will be hounded to the very gates of hell. The cartel bosses as well as their lieutenants will be decimated in an all-out push by the Mexican army. A push that has thus far been restrained by politicians concerned about ceding too much power to the military."

It took Nash only a second to see the rest of the plan, and it wasn't half bad. "You're going to make sure those other missiles are found in the possession of the cartel bosses you most want eliminated?"

Munoz smiled. "Exactly. My whole plan

revolves around letting the authorities wipe out the existing leadership structure of the major Mexican cartels, then stepping into the leadership void after the smoke has cleared. And you're going to help me do that by not only shooting down Mora's plane but also getting the other missiles in the right places to be found afterward."

Yeah, like that was going to effing happen.

"And what will we be doing during this purge?" Nash asked.

There was a certain brilliance to Munoz's scheme. Psychotic but brilliant.

Munoz took a long puff of his cigar and sat back with a sigh. "The first phase is already in motion. We've been collecting up and hiding away stockpiles of the weapons, ammunition, and explosives that we'll need once the dust settles. After that, the next part of the plan is simple. Once the dominos fall, all we have to do is sit back, enjoy the show, and focus on taking our operations international."

"It seems like you have this all planned out," Nash said. "But none of those dominoes start falling until we finish the deal for those missiles. Has Roman told you when they're supposed to arrive?"

"Tomorrow morning," Munoz said. "We'll

handle the final details of the deal then begin planning for phase two of the operation." He leaned forward and nudged the briefcase full of cash in his direction. "Assuming of course that you're going to take my offer. The ball is in your court, as you Americans like to say."

CHAPTER

"WHAT ARE YOU SO HAPPY ABOUT?" ISABELLA ASKED when Bristol walked into the kitchen.

After putting all the first-aid stuff away in the linen closet, she'd followed her nose to the kitchen where Isabella was making her famous chiles rellenos. No one made Poblano chiles stuffed with pork like Isabella. It was one of the things Bristol had missed when she'd been in college.

Bristol smiled as she walked over to the fridge. "What makes you think I'm happy?"

Isabella looked up from the sauce she was making to eye her appraisingly. "Because you were humming to yourself as you walked in and now you're grinning from ear to ear."

Bristol was still trying to come up with an answer to that when Isabella's eyes narrowed suspiciously. "And why are your lips so red?"

Bristol lifted her fingers to her lips, half hiding another grin at the reminder of the amazing kiss she and Nick had shared a few minutes ago. She'd never been kissed so passionately before. Apparently, making out like that with a guy like him left a mark on a girl's skin...and her heart as well.

A knowing smile spread across Isabella's face. "You've been kissing that man of yours, haven't you?"

Bristol took out a pitcher of homemade iced tea. "And if I was? Is there something wrong with two people kissing each other if they want?"

Isabella shook her head, her smile fading a little as she continued to stir the sauce. "Of course not, mija. As long as you know what you're getting yourself into. I know you can take care of yourself, but I still don't want to see you get hurt."

Bristol opened her mouth to tell Isabella she was worrying about nothing, but then closed it again. She poured the tea into a tall glass, then put the pitcher back into the fridge before turning to face Isabella. How could she fault her friend for saying the same thing she'd been thinking herself? At least up until she and Nick had made out in the bathroom a few minutes ago.

"I'm not going to get hurt," she said. "You can think I'm crazy if you want, but when I'm with Nick, I feel things that I've never felt before. And when he says he'll do everything he can to keep me safe and make sure my father pays for what he did to my mother, I believe him."

Isabella blinked in surprise. "You told him what happened to your mother? What Señor Munoz did to her?"

Bristol nodded. "At the beach yesterday. I wasn't planning for it to come out, but once we started talking..." She shrugged. "Nick is an easy man to trust. Pretty crazy, huh?"

She expected Isabella to tell her she'd been foolish, that revealing information like that to a man she didn't know was careless, even dangerous.

But her friend shook her head and smiled. "Maybe not so crazy. Sometimes our heart can know what is true long before our heads discover it. You simply have to be willing to listen to what your instincts are saying and follow where they lead you. That's what your mother always used to do."

Bristol frowned at that. "And look where that

got her. I remember a time when Mom thought my father was charming, too. Then he betrayed her."

"Do you think something like that could happen with Nick?"

"No," Bristol said, then sighed. "At least I hope not. I can't be that wrong about him."

But even as she said those words, she had to wonder if she was setting herself up for heartbreak. When it came right down to it, what did she really know about Nick Chapman? And what if everything she thought she knew turned out to be a lie?

⚓

"Where are Roman and Santiago?" Nash asked.

He saw lots of Munoz's goons standing by the range's firing line a few hundred yards away, but no sign of their CIA team leader or his tattooed ATF sidekick. Then again, he also didn't see any indication that the Mexican army was somewhere nearby either. Not that he expected to. According to the plan they'd come up with last night, the cavalry wasn't supposed to come charging in until Munoz took possession of the missiles this morning.

Dalton gave him a worried look, but Shaw didn't look concerned at all. "They said something about wanting to talk to Munoz this morning before the weapons exchange. I think Roman is hoping to get some more information on Edein Gojkic and the crazy scheme Munoz has planned for the missiles. Personally, I think Roman's pissed that you figured everything out before he did."

"Or he's pissed Munoz offered you all that friggin' money," Dalton said, leaning back against one of the range buildings with his arms crossed. "I'm telling you. Somebody waves that much money in front of me and I'd have to at least think about it."

Nash knew Dalton was full of crap. His teammate wasn't the kind to sell out his integrity for any amount of money. He just liked to act as if he would. No, Shaw was right, at least a little. Roman, and Santiago, too, had been thrown for a loop when Nash had told them everything he'd learned. Roman was familiar with Edein Gojkic, but was shocked to hear the man was involved in arms dealing. Apparently, Edein had been a general in the Russian army, rising up through the ranks as a soldier's soldier, a true warrior. The thought that a man like him had ended up using his connections to turn a profit had clearly stunned Roman."

"I'm going to see if any of Munoz's men know what's taking so long," Shaw said. "The longer we stand around, the better the chances are that something goes wrong."

After the CIA agent left, Dalton stepped away from the building he'd been leaning against and looked at Nash. "You thinking the reason Roman and Santiago aren't here is because the CIA have decided against stopping Munoz's little war?"

Nash shrugged. He hated to admit it, but he'd been wondering the same thing. "I hope that's not it. When we talked last night, Roman was the first one to point out how many innocent people would die if Munoz was allowed to go through with this scheme."

"I hear a *but* in there somewhere," Dalton prodded.

"But I could see some politician types back in the States seeing this as a win-win," Nash said. "Munoz kills a corrupt Mexican army officer and the army retaliates by wiping out a good portion of the existing cartel organizations. Sure, thousands will get caught in the crossfire between the army and the cartel, but we both know there are people in the CIA who wouldn't lose a minute of sleep over that."

Dalton considered that. "What are we going to do if they don't show and there's no Mexican army out there ready to come riding to the rescue?"

Before Nash could answer, a rumbling sound behind them filled the air. Nash turned around just in time to see a big cargo truck coming their way. A fancy black sedan was right behind it with Leon in the front passenger seat. Nash could see two people sitting in the backseat, but he couldn't make out who they were. Hopefully, it was Munoz and Roman.

Nash threw a covert look Dalton's way before glancing at the hills and scrubby woods beyond. He'd feel a whole hell of a lot better about this if he knew for sure backup was out there somewhere.

"Get ready," he told Dalton as he started forward to meet the sedan. "Looks like this is going down, one way or the other."

"In that case, maybe you ought to take this," Dalton said, walking up behind him and discreetly slipping something into his hand.

Nash immediately recognized the feel of a small-frame automatic pistol. A 9mm or 380 caliber. He palmed the weapon and shoved it into his back pocket.

"Double-action, no safety, six rounds in the magazine, one in the pipe," Dalton added as he casually took up the position most people would expect a bodyguard to take, slightly ahead of Nash and off to the side.

"Where'd you get the gun?" Nash asked as Leon got out of the sedan. The guy's face was bruised up pretty good and from the way he moved, his ribs were sore. The look he threw Nash's way as he opened the back door on the passenger's side could have melted the paint off the sedan.

"I went out drinking with the other guards again last night," Dalton said softly. "One of them owed me a lot of money from the bet he made during your fight with Leon. He didn't have any cash, so we traded his debt for his back-up piece. I lost out on the deal, but I won't complain. You can never have too many guns."

Nash snorted. He'd have to get the complete story out of his friend at some point, but now wasn't the time. Munoz was already getting out of the sedan. Things were about to get interesting.

"It might be a shitty time to bring this up, but have you considered what you're going to do about Bristol?" Dalton asked as they walked. "I'm not a cop, but I get the feeling Munoz's villa is going to be swarming with Federales and soldiers within minutes of this crap kicking off. What if they take her in, too? She's the boss's daughter after all."

"Yeah, I've given it some thought," Nash admitted. That was an understatement. In reality, he'd spent half the night lying awake wondering how to pull this mission off and still get the girl. "As soon as we have this situation under control, I'm going to need you to cover for me."

"You don't even have to ask," Dalton said. "But what the hell are you going to do, kidnap her?"

"If I have to," Nash muttered. "Hopefully, it won't come to that. I just need to find a way to get her out of the compound before things go really bad so I tell her what the hell is going on."

"You think she'll go anywhere with you after she figures out you've been lying to her the whole time?"

That was the part that had kept Nash up last night. The thought of Bristol hating him when she learned the truth made his gut clench. "I don't know," he said as Shaw headed their way. "Maybe I should have talked to her last night."

"That would have been too risky and you know it," Dalton said. "She has every reason in the world to hate her father, but he's still blood. If she'd had a change of heart and decided to warn him, we'd have been screwed."

Nash knew his friend was right, which was why he'd ultimately kept his butt in his own bed with his mouth shut. But damn, he'd hate himself later if this all went bad and he lost Bristol.

"Is it just me or does Munoz looked pissed?" Shaw asked as he joined them.

Nash glanced at the cartel boss, wondering if maybe Roman had been forced to delay the final deal until the Mexican army had gotten into position. Making Munoz wait would definitely rile the man up. But then he saw that Munoz was standing behind the opened car door, one hand resting on the waistband of his dress pants and the big automatic pistol shoved in there.

As Leon walked around the car to open the door on that side, the hair on the back of Nash's neck stood on end. Every instinct in his body screamed that something bad was about to go down. All at once, a steady calm came over him like it always did when the shit was about to hit the fan.

"This is going sideways on us," he said softly.

"What are you talking about?" Shaw asked, his voice filled with concern.

Nash ignored him. "Dalton, when it starts, go for the SUV we came in. The driver left the keys in it. I'll cover you."

"Guys, someone want to fill me in here?" Shaw said in a low voice.

"Nash, there are a dozen guards out here, plus Leon and Munoz. When they start shooting, you ain't holding them off with that little .380 I gave you," Dalton said.

Shaw looked like he still had no idea what was going on, but he didn't ask for clarification. "Don't suppose either of you have another weapon?"

Nash opened his mouth to tell him they didn't but stopped when he saw Dalton stiffen. A few yards away, the last passenger had gotten out of the sedan. It took him a moment to understand what was bothering his teammate until he noticed that the dark-haired, brown-eyed man looked eerily familiar.

"Oh, shit," he muttered.

Stopping in mid-stride, Nash reached one hand behind his back for the gun in his pocket. How the hell had everything gone so wrong, so fast?

"Damn, you do look like me," Nick Chapman—the *real* Nick Chapman—shouted with a laugh. "It's almost a shame to shoot someone so good looking, but I'll get over it."

As he spoke, Chapman lifted a MAC-10 submachine gun and rested it on top of the open door.

Nash already had his small auto out and was taking slow, careful shots at Chapman, Leon, and Munoz even as Dalton darted for the SUV fifty feet away. Unfortunately, the doors on Munoz's sedan were armored and Nash's little .380 rounds barely even cracked the windows. Then Chapman's MAC-10 began chattering in short, choppy bursts and Shaw went down. Nash couldn't see how bad it was because he was too busy hitting the ground so he wouldn't get shot.

Nash fired the remainder of his magazine at Chapman, making the man duck for cover. But even as Nash crawled toward Shaw, he knew it was too late. He was out of ammo and there was no way he and Shaw would survive until Dalton reached the vehicle and got back here. Especially not since Munoz's men had pulled their weapons and were heading this way. Maybe Dalton would be smart and get himself out of there alive at least.

Nah. Dalton would come back for them even if it got his ass killed.

Nash heard the roar of an engine behind him and turned to see a bright red commercial Hummer speeding down the gravel road, blazing past Dalton and the SUV he still hadn't reached. The Hummer barely slowed as it hurtled into the middle of the biggest cluster of Munoz's men and scattered them before crashing into the front end of Munoz's sedan. The SUV slammed to a halt, glass shattering, Munoz and the others shouting as they ran for safety. Then the monstrous vehicle jerked into reverse and backed toward Nash and Shaw.

Nash didn't know who was driving the thing, but whoever it was, they sure as hell knew how to make an entrance and pull off a rescue.

CHAPTER
Nine

BRISTOL WAS ALMOST DANCING WITH EXCITEMENT AS she left her room that morning. She didn't give a damn about her father's business, but today it suddenly mattered. Today, the final shipments of weapons her father had bought were coming in, with the exchange set to happen at the gun range not far from the villa. Once it did, Nick would officially begin working for her father and she'd finally have someone else besides Isabella whom she could trust. Someone else who wouldn't lie to her. Someone else who had her back. A man who would finally take down her father. And maybe, just maybe, she'd have a man she could fall in love with and start a whole new life.

Who was she kidding? As crazy as it seemed, she'd already fallen for him.

Nick Chapman was *that* special.

She'd been too excited to sleep last night so she'd gone down to the library, curled up in her favorite chair and spent hours thinking about Nick and wondering what her mother would have thought of him. She'd started to doze off around four in the morning when she heard voices in the hallway. While Nick's wasn't among them, the men had said his name several times. Not sure why she'd done it, she slipped out of the library and followed at a distance, shadowing Roman and the heavily tattooed biker guy until they went into her father's office. Even though it was insane, she'd stood at the door and eavesdropped anyway, listening as the two men and her father discussed the future purchase of other weapons and the possibility of Munoz moving the center of his operation to Europe.

Roman had just asked her father if he'd be interested in hiring them full-time as he had Nick when footsteps echoed at the other end of the hallway. Not eager to get caught by one of her father's men, she'd hurried back to her room and crawled into bed.

Bristol was in the kitchen nibbling on a churro for breakfast and wondering when Nick would be back when Isabella ran in with a frantic look on her face.

"Nick Chapman is here!"

A silly burst of happiness surged through her. The weapons exchange had taken less time than she'd thought. That was good. Although she couldn't understand why Isabella seemed so agitated.

"Great!" Bristol said. "I was thinking about asking him to have lunch with me, but breakfast will work, too."

Isabella shook her head. "No, it's not great. I was outside near the guard barracks a few minutes ago and saw your father talking with a man who called himself Nick Chapman. But it wasn't *your* Nick Chapman."

Bristol frowned. Her friend was making no sense. "There are two Nick Chapman's here now?"

Isabella gave her a frustrated look. "No, there's only one Nick Chapman here, and the man you've been kissing isn't him. The real Nick Chapman showed up this morning and he's furious."

Taking the half-eaten churro from Bristol, Isabella tossed it on the counter and grabbed her hands, her face pleading. "Bristol, the man you've fallen in love with isn't Nick Chapman. I don't know who he is, but he's not the mercenary arms dealer you thought he was."

Bristol's first instinct was to tell Isabella she was wrong, that she'd misheard something. But Bristol knew that wasn't true. Isabella was too smart for that. She'd seen what she'd seen and heard what she heard. But what did it mean?

"If Nick isn't the man I thought he was, who is he?"

Isabella squeezed her hands tighter, shaking her head again. "Like I said, I don't know. But if I had to guess, I would say he's someone sent in to take out your father."

Bristol's heart raced. "Sent in by whom?" Bristol asked.

"I don't know," Isabella said. "Maybe someone higher up in the Amador cartel, or a rival cartel even. It could be Interpol or the US. It could be anyone."

Bristol's knees went weak as a horrible thought occurred to her. Maybe Nick's promise to protect her had been a lie. "Was anything that happened between us real?" she whispered. "Or was it simply a way for him to get to my father?"

"That's something only you can answer,"

Isabella said. "But you don't have a lot of time to decide."

"What do you mean?"

"Your father and the real Nick Chapman are going to the range for the weapon exchange, and from the way they were talking, I think they plan on killing *your* Nick." Isabella's mouth tightened. "Leon went with them."

Bristol suddenly felt like she couldn't breathe. The man she'd been falling for had deliberately lied to her. Why did she feel anything for him?

Because no matter what lies had been spoken, her heart knew that the feelings between them had been real.

"I have to help him," she said firmly.

Isabella nodded, already urging her toward the door. "Take one of the vehicles in the garage. You know where the keys are kept, right?"

Bristol knew. She'd seen the big rack of keys in the small office off to the side of the garage a hundred times. But knowing where the keys were and being able to get one of them were two completely different things. There was always at least one guard in that office at all times. And another one usually patrolling the front of the villa.

"I'll never get to those keys," she protested.

Isabella stopped at the door leading into the garage and turned to face her. "You will if I distract the guards first."

Bristol opened her mouth to argue, but Isabella motioned her to silence. "Don't even try it. I'll be fine. Go help Nick—or whoever he is. Once you get to him, you can go to my sister's house to hide until the two of you can figure out a way to get out of Manzanillo. But be careful. There isn't anyone in the city your father doesn't own."

Before Bristol could even thank her, Isabella slipped into the garage. A moment later, Bristol heard her telling the men she'd made her special huevos rancheros for breakfast and that they'd better come inside right then if they wanted some.

Bristol couldn't imagine how that could possibly work. Her father's men weren't that easy to distract. But a few moment later, she heard footsteps approaching the door. She barely had time to hide behind it before Isabella and three guards walked in and headed for the kitchen.

She darted out the door and into the garage, praying everyone in it had gone with Isabella. Based on the silence that met her as she gazed at the long rows of sparkling cars and trucks, she realized Isabella had really done it.

Bristol ran into the office, making a beeline for the key rack. She hesitated for a moment, wondering which vehicle to take. Her first instinct was to go for something small and inconspicuous, but then she remembered that getting a vehicle was only the beginning of this little rescue attempt. She still had to get off the property then save *her* Nick. Shooting might be involved.

Her stomach tensed at the thought of someone shooting the man she cared about, and she had to hold onto the counter to steady herself. Grabbing the big key on the end of the rack, she turned to leave when she spotted two scary looking rifles leaning in the corner. She had no idea how to fire the weapons, but she knew they might come in handy.

Taking both of them, she ran across the big garage to the monstrous, red military-style SUV her father adored. She was terrified at the idea of driving something that big, but she knew it was powerful, fast for its size, and best of all, bulletproof.

Bristol tossed the two weapons on the center console of the vehicle, then climbed in. Quickly adjusting the seat so she could reach the pedals, she started the vehicle with a deep throated rumble, but then had to waste endless seconds trying to figure out what to do with all the different gearshift looking things beside her right knee. Knowing she didn't have time to mess around, she shoved one into drive and prayed the other two weren't important.

The heavy vehicle lurched forward, so she'd guessed right. Flooring the gas pedal, she squawked out of the garage, almost losing control before she straightened out and headed for the front gate. The guard there tried to block her path, but he chickened out soon enough, throwing himself to the side as Bristol crashed through the metal gates. She barely felt the impact.

The drive to the range seemed to take forever. She spent half the time looking behind her to see if anyone was following her and the other half fighting the big steering wheel as she tried to go as fast as she could. She had no idea how far ahead her father was, but all she could think of was what it would mean for her Nick if she was too late.

She was barely in control of the vehicle as she took the last turn onto the range. Her heart almost died at what she saw. Dalton was running toward a vehicle he was never going to reach before getting shot, while her Nick was on the ground with

Shaw as her father and the real Nick Chapman were shooting to kill.

Bristol punched the gas and drove right past her Nick, dispersing the crowd of guards and crashing into her father's sedan. The impact slammed the lighter vehicle backward, taking her father and the real Nick with it. While the shooting might have stopped for the moment, it wouldn't stay that way for long.

Putting the big SUV in reverse, she quickly backed up, then stopped and hopped out of the Hummer. The last time she'd seen her Nick he was on the ground. Could he walk? Was he even alive? Terror shot through her and she almost stumbled as she ran toward the rear of the vehicle. She'd barely gone two steps when her Nick ran around it, dragging Shaw with him. Blood stained the left leg of the man's jeans, and his face was contorted in pain.

Her Nick's eyes widened when he saw her, like he'd expected someone else to be driving the Hummer. He motioned for her to get in the SUV, then opened the back door and practically tossed Shaw into the backseat.

"I'll drive," he said, climbing into the driver's seat and urging her over the center console into the passenger seat. She got her seatbelt on just as Dalton jumped into the backseat besides Shaw.

Her Nick put it in reverse and floored it, backing up the Hummer a few hundred feet before slinging it around to get them pointed in the right direction. Then he took off, driving even faster than she had on the way in.

Bristol opened her mouth to ask him what the hell was going on and what his real name was, but Dalton leaned forward, blocking her view of the man she was pretty sure she was in love with and grinning like he was having the time of his life.

"Completely bitchin' entrance, Bristol. Slamming into your daddy's Mercedes really saved our asses." Dalton glanced down at the weapons, his eyes going wide. "You brought guns? Oh, that is friggin' too much! Nash, if you don't marry this woman right now on the spot, I'm going to do it myself."

"Nash?"

Bristol's voice was soft, almost tentative as he maneuvered the big Hummer along the curvy coastal road toward town. The hurt and pain in her voice tore at his gut, but this really wasn't the time or place to get into it. Not until they could get off the streets and find somewhere to hide. Unfortunately, doing that in a big, red SUV while hauling a bleeding CIA agent in the backseat was going to be tough. They kind of stood out.

"Is that your real name?" she prompted.

The wary look in Bristol's beautiful eyes just about did him in and he couldn't ignore the question.

"Yeah. Nash Cantrell...that's me." He darted a quick look at the rearview and caught sight of two black SUVs closing on them fast. He floored the gas, glancing at Bristol. "I guess you've figured out that I'm not the real Nick Chapman, huh?"

Bristol nodded.

"Yet you came to help me anyway," he pointed out. "You drove right into the middle of a gunfight for a man you couldn't be sure you could trust. Why?"

Bristol didn't say anything for a moment. "I couldn't stand the thought of you getting hurt. Even after I realized you lied to me."

"I never lied," he said. "I didn't tell you everything because I couldn't. But what I did tell you wasn't lies."

"You told me that you were a mercenary and an arms dealer," she accused him. "That's not true, is it?"

"I never actually said I was either of those things." In the review mirror, the SUVs were getting closer. He wasn't going to be able to outrun them. "I told you I was a SEAL just doing SEAL things, like jumping out of planes and landing on ships when I ended up working with people I didn't know, doing things I'd never imagined doing. I even told you that sometimes it felt like it was all make believe. That was true, every word of it. I'm an active duty Navy SEAL from San Diego they brought on this mission at the last second because I look like the real Nick Chapman."

Bristol stared at him, like she really wanted to believe him. "You're a US Navy SEAL. Seriously?"

Nash started to answer, but Dalton leaned forward and interrupted. "Yes. he's a SEAL and I'm a SEAL. Shaw is CIA with *real* CIA blood leaking out of him. And we have two bogeys coming up on our tail really fast. Now that we have the important facts out on the table, any chance we can skip the rest and focus on the part where we get out of this alive?"

Nash threw a quick glance over his shoulder. Dalton had torn the sleeves off his shirt and used them to bind the wound on Shaw's leg. There was some blood soaking through the bandages already, but it didn't look too bad. The agent was in pain, but he'd survive. At least as long as the rest of them, however long that might be.

He turned back to find Bristol regarding him thoughtfully. "You said you were from Brussels."

"No, I didn't. I said I couldn't remember the last time I was there. And that sometimes it felt like I've never been there. That was the truth. I've never been there."

"What about your family?" she demanded. "Did you really grow up in Colorado?"

"Yup. I'd never lie about family."

She nodded, and he thought he might finally be getting through to her. But the moment was lost as automatic weapons' fire slammed into the back of the vehicle, clanging against metal and bulletproof glass.

Nash glanced at Dalton. "If I let them get closer, any chance you can slow them down a little?"

Dalton snorted as he loaded the small Mexican HM-3 carbine that had been on the center console.

"It'll be difficult since I can't roll down the windows or shoot out the back like in a military Hummer, but I'll figure out a way to get it done."

Nash slowed down. A moment later, he heard a door open and he looked back in time to see Dalton lean out of the vehicle with Shaw holding onto his legs. The rapid chatter of gunfire filled the air and the windshield of one of the vehicles behind them shattered. It spun off the road and into the ditch in a slow-motion roll. The second vehicle pulled back a bit, not so eager now that someone was shooting back at them.

Nash turned his attention back to the road and found Bristol leaning over the center console toward him.

"And the kisses?" she asked, her face intent. "Were those for real or just part of the make believe, too?"

"Seriously?" Shaw grunted. "Is now the time for this?"

Both he and Bristol ignored the interruption.

"I think you already know the answer to that question," Nash said. "I wasn't planning to fall for you like I did. But when it happened, I wasn't going to act like there wasn't something there."

He was ready to say more, anything he needed

to convince her that what had transpired between them over the past few days was the realest thing he'd ever felt. But then she smiled at him and that derailed his thought processes faster than he would have ever thought possible.

"You've fallen for me?" she asked.

Another burst of gunfire smacked into the back of the Hummer. This time the bulletproof glass started to fracture a little. A few more hits and those bullets would be coming into the cab with them.

"Damn," Dalton said, leaning back in the vehicle with his weapon. "Could you two just admit you love each other and get it over with already?"

Nash started to say that he wasn't in love with Bristol, that he couldn't possibly be in love with any woman he'd only met a few days ago, but the words got hung up in his throat. Maybe the impossible wasn't quite as impossible as he thought.

Beside him, Bristol looked equally stunned, like maybe she'd been struck dumb by the same thought. Maybe Dalton was right. Not that Nash was ever going to admit it.

Suddenly, Nash desperately wanted to be alone with Bristol so he could find out exactly what was going on in her head and tell her what he was thinking, too. But before they could do that they needed to get rid of this last bad guy on their tail.

"Hold on," he said.

Slamming on the brakes, he slid to a stop in the middle of the road, then grabbed the other carbine from the center console and jumped out of the Hummer.

The vehicle following them tried to slow, but they were already too close for that. Nash lit them up. A split-second later, Dalton did the same. The hood blew up with a gout of flame and smoke, and the black SUV drove off the edge of the road without even slowing. It bounced and tumbled down toward the beach, but Nash didn't wait for it to come to a stop. He jumped back in the Hummer and got the big vehicle moving again, his mind already focused on what they had to do next.

First, they needed to find a place to hide. Second, they needed to deal with Shaw's injuries. And third, they needed to get on a phone to San Diego and get help down here.

"There's a small road to the left a few miles up," Bristol said, as if reading his mind. "I know someone who will help us hide until we can figure out what to do next."

CHAPTER
Ten

B RISTOL SAT ON THE BED AND WATCHED NASH WASH up in the adjoining bathroom. She liked his real name so much better. It fit him better than Nick.

"Where'd you learn to do all that?" she asked. "I know some first-aid, but you looked like a doctor down there."

Nash chuckled as he scrubbed the bar of soap all the way up to his elbow. "Hardly. The SEALs trained me to be a combat medic so I do okay with gunshot wounds and other major traumas. But I'm not even close to being a doctor."

Bristol wasn't sure of that. She'd never met a man who looked more calm and sure of himself as Nash had been when he'd dug a bullet out of Shaw's leg fifteen minutes ago. The fact that he'd done it on a kitchen table without any medical equipment only made it more impressive.

Rinsing the soap off his hands, Nash dried them on one of the freshly washed towels Isabella's sister, Josefina, had put out for him, then came back into the room. Shaw was resting in one of the bedrooms on the first floor, and Dalton was in the kitchen with Josefina helping her make something for all of them to eat.

"We're lucky Isabella has family that lives close." Nash picked up the cell phone he'd borrowed from Shaw from the night table and sat down on the bed beside Bristol. "And that Josefina was willing to help us."

Bristol had never doubted Isabella's sister would help them. She was only glad Josefina's husband and two sons were out fishing in Cuyutlan Bay and wouldn't be back until tomorrow. They were even more fortunate that Josefina was prone to seasickness and had stayed home. Hiding the Hummer in the barn and getting into the house would have been a lot more difficult if everything had been locked up.

"Who are you calling?" she asked as he dialed the phone.

All kinds of crazy thoughts ran through her head as she envisioned him calling in the CIA or the U.S. Navy. In truth, she had no idea how this kind of undercover thing worked. Were Nash and Dalton on their own now that their cover was blown? That seemed to be the way it happened in the movies.

"The Chief of my SEAL Team. He's the only person I trust in a situation like this."

Bristol listened as Nash talked to someone named Chasen, telling the other man how he and Dalton had been dropped into an undercover mission in Mexico, that it had all gone bad, and where they were now. Though she could only hear Nash's side of the conversation, it seemed his chief took the news in stride. Maybe SEALs were in situations like this all the time.

"I'm pretty sure Roman and Santiago are both dead," Nash told Chasen. "It's the only thing that explains why we haven't seen or heard from either of them since early this morning. It also explains how the real Nick Chapman was able to get free and why the Mexican army never showed up at the weapons exchange."

On the way here, Bristol had told Nash about the conversation she'd overheard outside her father's study last night. It had only strengthened his suspicions that somehow the two American

agents had screwed up and revealed their iden-
tities, and that her father had killed them as a
result.

Nash gave Chasen the address of Josefina's
farm, promising to stay put until backup arrived,
then hung up and tossed the phone on the night
table. "Chasen is going to get in contact with the
CIA and let them know what's happening, then
get some of my teammates down here to help get
us out."

Bristol did a double take. Did he mean him
and Dalton or was he including her, too? "Us?"

Nash frowned. "What did you think? That I
was going to leave you here to deal with your father and Leon on your own?"

Her heart beat a little faster. She hadn't been
entirely sure what to think. And she'd been afraid
to assume anything regardless of what Nash said
on the drive there about everything between them
being real. "Will you be able to get me into the US
without my American passport?"

"That's not a problem. I know some people
who can talk to the State Department for me." He
regarded her expectantly. "I was kind of thinking
you could come back to San Diego with me. If you
want to, I mean."

Her heart began to race so fast she thought it might explode. "With you?"

Mouth curving into a smile, Nash traced his thumb lightly along her jawline. "Like I told you in the Hummer, I'm not the kind of guy who's going to act like there's nothing between us when I know there is. And since we can't stay here to see where it goes, I thought you might want to come home with me so we can figure it out there."

Bristol closed her eyes, covering Nash's hand with her own where it rested against her face, wanting to experience this moment for a little while. She'd spent a good portion of last night daydreaming about what it would be like to find out that Nash felt the same way about her that she felt about him. It had been more wishful thinking than anything else. She didn't want to jinx anything by putting the cart before the horse, but a few tears slipped out at the realization that maybe her wish could really come true.

She opened her eyes to find Nash still wearing that sexy grin. "I hope those are tears of happiness or I'm going to feel pretty damn foolish."

She laughed. "Yes, they're tears of happiness. It's just that this is all so much to take in."

Nash moved his hand slightly burying his

fingers into the hair at the nape of her neck, gently tugging her forward until their foreheads were touching. "Hey, it's okay. I promise I won't rush you into anything. We can take things at your pace."

"I know." She gazed deep into his eyes, loving the sensation of being so close to him. "It's not about you rushing me. It's about me wanting this so badly."

His lips brushed against hers, his warm breath caressing her skin and making her shiver. "I want this, too."

She tipped her face up, kissing him back. His tongue slipped into her mouth to slow dance with hers, and she moaned softly. Nash tightened his hand in her hair, holding her firmly as his tongue teased and explored. Damn, he could kiss.

Bristol wasn't sure when she decided this was going further than a kiss, but suddenly her hands were under his T-shirt, her fingers running up his ripped abs, pushing the material higher. Nash pulled back, breaking the kiss and pulling his shirt off.

"You sure about this?" he asked softly. "I don't have a condom on me. I wasn't exactly thinking I'd need one today."

She laughed, gliding her palms upward along his deeply muscled pecs to his broad shoulders and strong neck. It was nice being with a man who cared about stuff like that. "As far as a condom, I'm in the safe part of my cycle for another four days, so that's not an issue. I also got tested for STD's before I came back to Mexico. Since then, I haven't slept with anyone. And as far as being sure, I'm more sure about this than I've ever been about anything. I know we don't have to rush, but that doesn't mean we have to go slow either. I want this...and I want you."

Nash relaxed and pulled her close again, his mouth coming down on her neck, warm lips tracing fire all the way from her collar bone to her earlobes. "Not as much as I want you. And in the interest of full disclosure, I've been tested, too."

She smiled and reached for his belt. "Then what are we waiting for?"

Chuckling, Nash stood to shove down his jeans. Bristol blinked. Damn, she'd never seen a man so perfect. Long muscular legs, abs and pecs that seemed to be carved from stone, and biceps and shoulders that made her mouth water with a crazy urge to nip and nibble them.

She leaned back on the bed and watched as he

skimmed down his tight underwear, her breath catching in her throat at the sight of his shaft. Yeah, that part of him was perfect, too. Long, thick, and best of all, hard.

It almost made her giddy to think she was the reason he was so excited.

She kicked off her shoes and grabbed the bottom of her top, eager to get out of her clothes now that he was naked, but Nash's voice stopped her.

"I probably don't need to say this, but there are people downstairs. Keep that in mind later when you feel the urge to scream."

She lifted a brow. "You think that's a possibility?"

He reached out and grabbed her ankles, dragging her toward the edge of the bed and making her laugh. "You'll want to scream. I can guarantee that."

Her jeans ended up in a heap on the floor, quickly followed by her shirt, bra, and panties. When she was completely naked, Nash stood taking her all in like she was the most beautiful woman in the world. The expression on his face, half awe, half smoldering heat was almost enough to make her blush.

Nash offered his hand and she took it, letting

him pull her off the bed and to her feet. She immediately melted into his arms, luxuriating in the feel of his hard, muscular body pressing against her softer curves. Bristol dropped a hand down to wrap around his erection, caressing softly as his fingers found their way into her hair and his mouth came down to capture hers.

Bristol lost herself in the moment, surrendering to the sensations of his warm mouth stealing her breath, his strong hand sliding down her back to cup her butt, his cock throbbing in her hand.

She could stay right there forever.

But Nash obviously had other ideas. Slowly pulling away, he turned her around until she was facing away from him. Then he wrapped his arms around her waist, tugging her to him so that his erection was nestled firmly against her ass.

She leaned back into him, grinding her bottom a little as he pressed a hot kiss to the curve of her neck. Nash's right hand glided down her stomach and she instinctively spread her legs a little, biting her lower lip when his fingers skimmed her wet folds.

Nash seemed to be deliberately trying to tease her because he skillfully avoided her clit as he repeatedly slid his middle finger deep inside then out. Her legs quivered, and if she hadn't been holding onto his arm around her middle she probably would have melted into a puddle on the floor.

When he finally got around to caressing her clit, her body spasmed like she'd touched a live wire. The tingling between her legs gradually got more intense, a sure indication she was going to come soon. She took a deep breath in anticipation and reminded herself not to scream.

Then Nash took his finger away, and she almost did scream, this time in frustration. She groaned in protest, but he shushed her, his breath tickling her ear as he cupped her breasts and played with her nipples. Since it felt so amazing, she couldn't really complain. That said, she still wanted to shout for joy when he once more slid his hand between her legs to finger her again. She rotated her hips in time with his movements, loving the feel of his hardness against her ass almost as much as his touch on her clit.

When her breath began to come in quick pants and her body started to tense up, she was half afraid he was going to pull his hand away, but he only squeezed her tighter and quickened his movements, drawing the climax from her in a rush that made her whole body shake. She clenched the arm wrapped around her and bit her lip again, trying desperately not to cry out.

Nash whispered in her ear the whole time she was coming, though she couldn't make out any of it. All she could do was moan.

Bristol wasn't sure how long her orgasm lasted. Nash was an expert at teasing the pleasure out of her long after she thought it was over. She didn't even realize he'd picked her up in his arms and set her down on the edge of the bed until he stepped between her spread legs. She wrapped them around him, tugging him closer.

"No more teasing," she whispered as he rubbed the thick head of his shaft up and down her slick folds.

Gaze locked on hers, he grasped her hips, then slowly eased into her. Even though she was more than ready for him, she still gasped when he filled her. No man she'd ever been with had ever felt this perfect.

As he thrust, Nash ran his hands over her hips and up her tummy to cup her breasts. He lingered there, playing with her nipples as he pushed her closer and closer to another orgasm. While Bristol was definitely a fan of the slow and gentle approach, she needed all of him—now.

"Harder," she whispered.

He immediately slid his hands down to grasp her hips again, pumping into her faster. "Like this?"

All she could do was moan in reply. She knew she should be quiet, but that wasn't going to be possible. Not with Nash doing incredible things to her body like this.

Her climax built higher and higher with every thrust. As the wave crested, Nash leaned forward to cover her mouth with his, stealing her breath away. She wrapped her arms and legs around him tightly, coming hard and feeling him come with her. It was the most glorious thing she'd ever felt.

When she floated down from her orgasmic high, Bristol realized Nash had slid her farther across the bed, making room so he could join her. He was still carefully resting his weight between her legs, his cock buried deep inside her.

"That was incredible," she whispered as he leaned forward to give her another kiss, this one softer and more tender. "I hope I wasn't too loud."

He chuckled, leaving a trail of kisses along her jaw and down her neck. "You weren't. But we just started so I still have a few more chances to make you scream."

Heat pooled between her thighs as he moved his mouth lower, capturing one of her very sensitive nipples between his lips and doing things to it that made her think Nash was going to make good on his promise.

Nash was in the kitchen making coffee when Shaw's phone rang. Nash quickly dug it out of his pocket and thumbed the green button. He loved spending time with Bristol, but after fourteen hours of sitting around on his hands waiting, he was getting a little antsy. He was a Navy SEAL. Doing nothing wasn't in his DNA.

"Cantrell," he said.

"It's me." On the other end of the line, Roman's voice was weak, his breathing labored. Damn, the senior CIA agent didn't sound good at all. "Are you someplace where you can talk?"

"Yeah. Hang on while I put you on speaker so Dalton can hear."

Nash strode into the living room where Dalton was in the middle of telling Bristol and

Josefina a story of one of his many escapades.

"You're on speaker, Roman," Nash said. "What happened? Are you hurt?"

There was a wet sounding cough. "I've been better. Where's Shaw? This is his phone."

"He's okay. Took one in the leg." Even though he was in bad shape, Roman was still more worried about his people than himself. That said something about a man. "Don't worry about him. Tell me where you are and I'll come get you. Is Santiago with you?"

"Santiago's dead." Roman let out another cough. "I don't know what happened. Munoz must have made us somehow. Leon was supposed to take us to the port to get the missiles, but we'd barely gone more than a mile or two from the villa when he pulled over at an abandoned house with blue stucco walls and lots of old thatching on the roof. He and the other guy with him shot Santiago and me without ever saying a word. I thought I was going to buy it, too, but I guess not."

Shit. That meant Roman had been unconscious for nearly an entire day. It was a miracle he'd woken up. There was no telling how much longer the man could hang on without medical treatment, though. Which meant he had to get there fast. Unfortunately, Nash wasn't sure if they'd be able to take Roman to a hospital. A gunshot would bring the police as fast there as in the States. But here, Munoz owned a lot of the cops.

"I know where he is," Bristol whispered. "It's about five miles from here. You can't miss it."

Nash nodded. "Roman, you hang tight. We know where you are and we'll be there in ten minutes."

Roman's laugh ended in a fit of coughing. "I'll be here. Not like I'm going anywhere."

Hanging up, Nash looked at Josefina. "Could I borrow your car?"

Even in the dark, that red Hummer would stick out like a sore thumb.

The woman nodded. "Of course. I'll get the keys."

"Let me grab my shoes," Bristol said, starting for the stairs.

Nash caught her arm. "I need you to stay here and keep an eye on Shaw."

She frowned. "Don't even try it. You don't want me to go because you think it might be dangerous."

"You're right. I don't." He sighed. "We could run into your father's men out there and I won't be able to focus on fighting them if you're there because I'll be too worried about you."

Fear flashed in Bristol's eyes. She grabbed his hand, holding it tightly. "Don't you think I'll be worried about you, too?"

Nash opened his mouth to answer, then closed it again. It suddenly dawned on him that he'd never had anyone worry about him before. Sure, his family did, but that was different. This was the woman he was falling for. It probably shouldn't have made any difference, but it did.

A few feet away, Dalton looking at him expectantly, knowing like Nash did that they didn't have time to waste.

"I know you're going to worry about me, Bristol," he said softly. "But I'm a SEAL. This is what I do. Not just here and now, but for the foreseeable future. I want us to be together, but that's something you need to accept. I'm going to be careful, and I have Dalton there to watch my back, but I need to go do this. And you need to let me."

She regarded him thoughtfully for a moment, but then nodded and looked away, blinking back tears she probably thought he couldn't see. "How are you going to find the house in the dark without me?"

He cupped her cheek, gently turning her face

to his. "You said we wouldn't be able to miss it, remember? But in case that was an exaggeration, maybe you could draw me a quick map?"

Bristol took a deep breath, then nodded again. "Okay. But you have to promise me that you'll be careful."

"I will." Nash kissed her gently on the lips. "I'll be back before you know it. I promise."

CHAPTER
Eleven

S HE'S GOING TO BE FINE." DALTON SAID AS HE DROVE the borrowed pickup truck along the coastal road as fast as he could without attracting too much attention. "There's no way in hell Munoz would ever figure out she's at Josefina's place."

"I know," Nash said, telling himself the twist he felt in his gut didn't mean anything. That he was worrying for no reason. "I'd just feel a lot better if Shaw was a bit more mobile. You left him your pistol, but it's not like he can do regular perimeter checks or anything like that."

"He won't have to. Especially if we find Roman and get back to the house quickly."

Nash hoped that was true. "You heard the way Roman sounded on the phone. You think there's even a chance he's still alive by the time we find him?"

Dalton shrugged. "We'll find out soon enough."

A few minutes later, they made a left turn and Nash spotted the cluster of palm trees near the edge of the road that Bristol described.

"The turn off should be coming up on the right," he told Dalton.

Thanks to Bristol's map, it wasn't difficult to find the abandoned house in the dark, even though it was well back from the road and half hidden by shrubs. Dalton turned off the engine and killed the lights, coasting to a stop halfway up the driveway to the house. Grabbing his weapon, Nash opened his door and got out, falling into step beside Dalton.

Nash flipped the selector on his assault weapon off safe and scanned the overgrown yard as he walked. The house was a big two-story structure with single story wings extending out to either side and most of the windows broken out. Other than the whisper of the palm trees swaying in the night breeze, it was as quiet as a tomb. Luckily, the sliver of moon high in the sky provided enough light to see, though if Roman was around there somewhere, he wasn't making his presence known. Then again, the guy might not even be conscious.

Nash motioned to Dalton to take lead around the right side of the house, following about twenty feet back to cover his teammate, while keeping most of his attention on the heavy brush that encircled nearly the entire back of the property. He didn't think there was anyone hiding back there, but his instincts and training made him wary of any place he couldn't see.

They were halfway across the back of the house and still no sight or sound of Roman. Dalton threw him a glance, and Nash knew exactly what his buddy was thinking.

Was the CIA agent still alive?

"Roman?" Nash called.

He hated the idea of announcing their presence, but he didn't have a choice.

Nash stopped, straining to hear something—anything—that might give them hope. A few feet ahead of him, Dalton did the same. After a full minute, Nash was ready to give up, but then he heard a soft cough coming from the back left corner of the house near the covered patio area. Dalton must have heard it, too because he immediately turned and headed that way.

"Hold on, Roman!" Nash jogged to catch up

with Dalton. "We're coming."

They were twenty feet away from the patio when Nash caught a flash of movement out of the corner of his eye. He whipped around to see moonlight glinting off metal behind one of the broken windows on the second floor.

"Ambush left!" he shouted, launching himself forward and to the right, knowing Dalton would do the same without asking questions

Automatic weapon fire pierced the night, echoing in the darkness. A split second later, more rounds came from the bushes along the back of the property.

Nash hit the ground rolling as bullets tore up the ground around him. He got under the patio cover seconds before the rounds ripped into the dirt he'd been hugging. He jumped to his feet, ready to return fire toward the second floor as Dalton focused on whoever was shooting at them from the rear of the property when a shadowy figure came out from behind a built-in barbecue pit on the far side of the patio.

Nash whipped around, almost firing in that direction, but stopped when the man stepped forward into a beam of moonlight coming through the vine-covered pergola. Relief coursed through

Nash even as bullets continued to rain down all around them.

"Roman. How the hell are you still alive?"

Nash started toward the injured CIA agent when he caught the hard look in his eyes. That was when he caught sight of the pistol in Roman's hand.

Alarms bells went off, and Nash's stomach clenched as he realized they'd been tricked. Cursing, he pulled the trigger on the compact submachine gun in his hand. Roman must have anticipated the move because he ducked behind the barbecue pit. That was more than enough time for Nash to bail.

"Dalton, go!" he yelled as he raced toward the French doors standing between him and the interior of the house. He got there first, smashing through the wood and glass, rolling as he hit the tile floor beyond. Dalton came in right behind him, and they both scrambled for cover. Dalton slid behind a heavy island in the center of the kitchen while Nash took cover near the wall beside the doors. Bullets smacked into the tile floors, ricocheting off the walls, bits of plaster and clay going everywhere.

"There are two upstairs," he told Dalton.

"Yup." Dalton calmly dropped the magazine on his carbine and checked to see how many rounds he had left. "I'm guessing they'll be coming down to visit soon. You deal with the ones outside. I'll handle the ones inside."

Nash nodded, peeking around the door frame. Roman was out there with two other men. One of them Gerard Santiago.

Son of a bitch.

"You know Roman betrayed us, right?" he asked Dalton. "This whole thing was a trap from the get go."

Dalton snorted. "Yeah, I kind of figured that out. But you have to admit, he sounded convincing as hell on the phone. Don't feel bad about buying his bullshit. I did, too."

Getting up, Dalton darted down a hallway that looked like it headed toward the back of the house and hopefully the stairs.

Nash caught sight of Santiago and one of Munoz's men moving to the right while Roman stayed where he was. No doubt the asshole was planning to distract Nash while the other two men slipped into the house and tried to take him out from behind.

"You should have taken Munoz up on that

offer," Roman shouted. "You could be sitting on a briefcase full of money right now instead of heading for a shallow grave."

"One briefcase of cash. Is that all it took for you to sell out your country?" Nash yelled back.

He was only paying partial attention to the CIA agent. Most of his focus was on the sound of footsteps on broken glass on the right side of the house. Those two idiots probably thought they were being stealthy. They weren't.

"Hell, yeah!" Roman laughed. "I've been living undercover like a criminal getting shot at, knifed, and beaten up for the better part of twenty-five years, and for what? That one briefcase is more money than I'll see in my life."

"And what did you and Santiago have to do to earn all that money besides rat Dalton and me out?" Nash demanded.

The footsteps were coming closer. This little ambush was going to be over with in the next few seconds, one way or the other.

"Giving you two up was a freebie," Roman said. His voice was closer now. Probably so he could charge in the moment the shooting started. "What Munoz really wanted was access to the CIA and ATF. With us feeding him intel from the inside, he figured it would be easy to stay one step ahead of the people coming after him."

"And what about Shaw?" Nash asked, darting across the kitchen and taking up a position to the side of the entryway Santiago and the other guy would use. "You decided not to cut him in on the deal?"

"Yeah. I felt a little bad about that. But Shaw's too young and naive to ever consider a deal like this. So, he had to go. Just the price he had to pay, I guess."

"You must be pissed he's still alive." Nash said, lifting his weapon and waiting.

One of two things was about to happen...either Santiago and his buddy would rush into the kitchen and try to surprise him. Or they'd move in slowly, thinking they'd shoot him in the back as he talked to Roman. He was betting on the former. Santiago didn't seem like the slow and patient type.

"I'm not too worried about Shaw," Roman said from just outside the French doors. "There's someone taking care of that problem right now."

Realization hit Nash like a Mack tuck. He had about a half second to curse before a hail of gunfire cut loose upstairs. Santiago burst into the kitchen, the other guard right behind him. The men sprayed the room with bullets as they moved, unaware that Nash was behind them.

Nash didn't think. He just pulled the trigger, hitting both men multiple times. He didn't wait for them to hit the floor before spinning to face the door. Roman charged in on cue, bullets blazing. Nash ignored the rounds smashing into the walls and cabinets around him, calmly putting a three-round burst into the other man's chest.

Roman slid halfway across the kitchen before thumping into the island and coming to a stop. Nash threw a quick glance at Santiago and the other man to make sure they were staying down before moving across the floor to kneel down by Roman.

He jerked the man onto his back, hoping to ask him what the hell he'd meant about Shaw, but it was too late for that. All three of the 9mm rounds Nash had fired had hit vital locations. Roman had been dead before he'd hit the floor.

"You okay?" Dalton asked from behind him.

"Yeah, I'm good." Getting to his feet, Nash collected up the weapons and all the ammo he could find on the three corpses. "We need to get back to the house. This whole thing was a ruse to get us to leave Shaw and Bristol alone."

⚓

Nash was out of the truck and running for the front door before Dalton had even brought the vehicle to a stop in Josefina's driveway. His heart stopped when he found the door ajar. His worst fears had been right. Munoz had sent men here to deal with Shaw—and Bristol—while he and Dalton had been screwing around with Roman.

Shit.

Jaw clenched, he drew the handgun he'd taken from Roman and cautiously moved through the house, taking in the two dead men on the floor, the tipped-over couch, the broken lamp, and the bullet holes in the walls. There had been a lot of people in here, and Shaw had fought back.

He found Shaw and Josefina in the kitchen. The CIA agent was sitting on the floor leaning against the refrigerator, blood covering the front of his shirt and running from the bandage around his leg. Josefina was beside him holding a towel pressed to the wound near his shoulder. There was a handgun on the floor near Shaw's leg, the upper receiver locked back...empty. And no sign of Bristol.

Shaw shook his head when he saw Nash. "I'm sorry," he gasped. "I tried to stop them, but there were too many."

Nash pushed thoughts of Bristol aside for the moment—as hard as that was to do—and dropped down on one knee beside Shaw. He ripped open Shaw's shirt to reveal a bloody wound through the upper part of his chest directly below his left collarbone. It was bad, but not fatal. Not in the short term at least. Nash wadded up a piece of Shaw's shirt, pressing it against the wound, staunching the flow of blood. But stopping the bleeding was just the start.

"A leg wound was one thing, but this is different," Nash said. "I can't deal with something like this with some antiseptic and a bandage. You'll need a doctor. Someone we can trust."

"I know someone who will help us," Josefina said. "And they're not connected to Munoz."

Shaw tried to push Nash's hand away so he could get up. When Nash didn't move, the CIA agent slid back down to the floor.

"Leon and two of Munoz's men took Bristol less than ten minutes ago, Nash. We both know where they're taking her. I can help get her back."

He probably would have said more, but Dalton came in right then...with company. Nash looked up and saw Wes, Holden, Logan and Trent. The sight of them was like a huge weight had been lifted off his shoulders.

Josefina took over with the makeshift bandage, giving Nash a nod.

Straightening, he walked over to meet his buddies. "How much do you already know?"

He didn't want to waste time filling them in if he didn't need to. Shaw was right. Nash knew exactly where they'd taken Bristol. He also knew what would happen to her when she got there. The same thing that had happened to her mother.

"Dalton already caught us up on the important details," Logan said. Tall with dark blond hair and blue eyes, he was one of the Team's petty officers. "He told us Bristol is important to you, that her father is a psychopath with a lot of goons and a lot of weapons, and that we're going to help rescue her. Oh yeah, he also mentioned that the CIA and ATF agents running this operation took a bribe and sold you all out."

"What?" Shaw demanded.

Nash ignored him. Instead, he threw a look of appreciation at Dalton. "That's pretty much the basics. Now tell me you brought weapons with you? We have a handful of crap-stuff we've collected recently, but not much in the way of ammo."

Logan shook his head. "Unfortunately, we don't. Headquarters was seriously against sending anyone down here in an official capacity, preferring to leave this mess squarely in the hands of the CIA. Chasen got us down here on leave, but that meant commercial flights. We tried to get our tactical vests and night vision goggles through security, but even that was a no-go."

Nash cursed, then glanced at Josefina. "Can you take care of Shaw on your own?" At the older woman's nod, he turned back to Dalton. "I know where we can get as many weapons as we need—and then some."

Dalton grinned. "Munoz's gun range."

"Exactly," Nash said. "But we don't have time to screw around so let's get the hell over there."

CHAPTER
Twelve

I T'S NOT YOUR FAULT." BRISTOL SAT ON THE FLOOR IN THE same bedroom where she'd tended to Nash's wounds, cradling Isabella in her lap. She gently brushed Isabella's hair out of her face. "Leon is a monster. If you hadn't told him where I was, he would have killed you."

"I should have let him," Isabella whispered. "At least then he wouldn't have gotten you. Or hurt my sister."

Isabella's words came out a little slurred courtesy of the split lip and swelled jaw Leon had given her. Along with the bruises that covered the rest of her body. For the second time in as many days, Bristol'd had to use the first-aid supplies in the adjoining bathroom to tend to someone she cared about. Luckily, there'd been some over-the-counter pain relievers in there as well. The pills seemed to have helped Isabella some.

"Don't even talk like that," Bristol shushed her. "I'm fine and your sister's fine, too. Leon was too busy dragging me out of Josefina's house to bother with her. So, let's focus on getting away and not wasting time worrying."

Bristol hadn't mentioned that Leon had shot Shaw in the chest and left him for dead. Knowing that would only scare Isabella more, and Bristol wanted her focused on getting out of here. Unfortunately, while getting away was a great idea, Bristol had no idea how to make it happen. There were no windows in this part of the villa and the guard Leon had left outside the door over an hour ago still hadn't left.

The only real hope either of them had was that Nash would come to save them. But while she wanted to see Nash more than anything in the world, a huge part of Bristol prayed he wouldn't come. Her father had more men at the villa than Bristol had ever seen before. If Nash and Dalton showed up to rescue them, both of them would likely end up paying with their lives.

The same way her mom had paid when she'd tried to leave with Bristol.

Thinking of her mother made Bristol wonder

why she wasn't already dead. Her father knew she'd stolen the Hummer and rescued Nash and the other guys. Luis Munoz wasn't the kind of man to accept betrayal of any kind, and certainly not from his daughter. Maybe her father wanted to look her in the eye one more time before he ordered her execution.

Bristol was still trying to think of some way to escape when the door opened. Dread filled her when she saw Leon. Gently moving Isabella aside, she got to her feet to stand protectively in front of her friend. Well, as protectively as she could considering Leon was much bigger and stronger than she was.

"What do you want?" Bristol demanded.

The hatred she felt for Leon for what he'd done first to her mother, and now Isabella, made her voice stronger than she expected. In reality, she was terrified of him and whatever he planned to do to them.

"Your father wants to see you."

While his tone might have been casual, his eyes conveyed something completely different. They wandered over her with a lust in them that made Bristol feel like she needed to take a bath.

Something told her a trip to see her father

wasn't the only thing Leon had in mind for her. "I'm not going anywhere with you."

Leon shrugged. "Fine. Then I'll just finish what I started with Isabella."

"Stay away from her," Bristol ordered, intercepting him before he could get close to Isabella. "I'll go with you."

"Smart move," Leon said. "Let's go."

Bristol crouched down in front of Isabella. "I'll be back," she whispered. "I don't know how yet, but I'm going to get us both out of here."

Isabella looked doubtful. "Be careful, mija. Don't provoke your father. That was the mistake your mother made."

Bristol didn't tell Isabella that she'd already provoked him by siding with Nash. Instead, she nodded and turned to Leon.

As he led her to her father's study, Bristol glanced out the window to see men loading large wooden crates into several trucks in the driveway. The weapons her father had purchased.

Her father wasn't alone in his study. Nick Chapman was with him, seated in one of the chairs in front of the desk. The physical resemblance between him and Nash was almost eerie. But something told her that was where the similarities ended. There were two metal briefcases on the desk filled with stacks of American money.

From where he sat behind the desk, her father regarded her coldly. "Sit."

She almost told him she'd rather stand, but then thought better of it. She knew she'd lose in a battle of wills. Moreover, Leon was still beside her. He looked like he was just waiting for her to refuse.

Taking a deep breath, she slipped into the chair next to Chapman. Leon smirked.

"You're too much like your mother for your own good," her father said. "She was naive, too, thinking she could walk away from me without paying a price."

She glared at her father, anger boiling up inside her. "So, you had her killed simply because she wanted to leave you?"

"I couldn't have people thinking I was weak, which they would have if I let her walk away. Though I should probably clarify one point. I didn't *have* her killed. I did it myself." He shrugged. "Leon was the one who ran her off the road near that abandoned villa with the blue stucco walls a few miles down the road. But I'm the one who looked your mother in the eyes and put a bullet in her. She's still there by the way, buried in the backyard."

Tears ran down Bristol's cheeks even though she tried to stop them. She hated that her father could see he'd gotten to her. She'd accepted a long time ago that her mother was dead, but hearing her father say the words exposed the fact that at least some secret part of her had held out hope. That was shattered now, destroyed by her father's admission that he'd been the one who murdered her and that her body was lying in an unmarked grave only a few miles from here.

That it was the same location where Nash and Dalton had gone to rescue Roman couldn't be a coincidence.

Her father smiled, triumph in his eyes. "Yes, Bristol. I know all about Nash and his friend, Dalton, going to that exact same villa to save the poor, wounded CIA agent. I was standing right beside Roman when the man gave that convincing performance on the phone. You have to appreciate the delicious symmetry though. Taking this new love away from you in the same place I took your mother away."

One moment Bristol was sitting there, the next she was throwing herself at her father, determined to tear him to shreds. She didn't get very far before Leon grabbed her and shoved her back down in the chair, holding her there with a firm hand on her shoulder. Fresh tears spilled onto her cheeks.

Nash wasn't dead. He couldn't be.

"Now that you realize you'll never have anything in this world unless I allow it, I'm ready to put all of this behind us," her father said.

Bristol glared at him through her tears. "Meaning?"

"I've offered Nick the same job that I offered Nash," he explained. "I even doubled the money."

"Why are you telling me this?" she asked.

"Because he wants you as part of the deal."

Bristol looked at Nick. He gave her a smug smile. If Leon hadn't been holding her down, she would have gone for his throat, too.

"If you agree, I'm willing to let bygones be bygones," her father added.

Bristol's heart died inside her then. She'd never see Nash again, never get to go to San Diego with him, or make love to him, or build a life with him...

On the wall behind her father's chair, her mother smiled down at her from the portrait.

"I'd rather die," Bristol said flatly.

"That can be arranged."

Her father made a flicking motion with his hand. Leon yanked her out of the chair and propelled her toward the door as her father turned his attention to Nick and whatever job he wanted the man to do, as if he didn't care she'd be killed within the hour. Why should he? She was already dead to him.

She considered begging Leon. Not for her own life, but for Isabella's. She decided not to bother. Leon wasn't human. Why would he do anything for her?

Bristol was surprised when Leon headed toward the front door. She assumed he'd take her out to the bluff overlooking the beach and shoot her right there. She supposed he was going to take her somewhere else to do it.

Maybe to the same place where her mother and Nash had been killed. That would be okay. Better even. A final resting place with the people she loved.

The men she'd seen loading the trucks earlier were still in the driveway and they stopped Leon to ask him where her father wanted certain weapons hidden. Leon must not have thought she would try to escape because he let her arm go as he explained to the men that most of the weapons and ammunition were going to be taken out of the city and moved south. Within moments, there was a good twenty feet between them. She thought she might be able to fade into the crowd and disappear, but then Leon turned and stabbed her with his angry glare and she knew she'd wasted her chance.

Suddenly, gunfire came from the direction of the bluff, as well as the stairs leading down to the beach and the dock. Her eyes widened as she saw a flaming fireball speeding toward the driveway. She had no idea what it was, but she knew it was dangerous.

She threw herself to the ground just as it hit the truck near Leon. There was a huge explosion and the heavily-loaded truck simply came apart. Men went flying in every direction, including Leon. The blast picked him up and tossed him through one of the windows of the villa like he was a toy.

Every instinct in Bristol told her to stay exactly where she was, but God had given her a second chance and she wasn't going to waste it.

She climbed to her feet, knowing two things. One, she had to rescue Isabella. And two, Nash was somewhere out there making all this happen.

CHAPTER

Thirteen

NASH HAD JUST CLIMBED OVER THE PERIMETER WALL OF Munoz's property with Dalton and started moving toward the villa when he caught sight of Bristol. Nash felt a sense of relief so overwhelming he actually got a little dizzy. She was surrounded by a lot of bad guys—including Leon—but she was alive, and that was all that mattered.

He and the other guys on his SEAL team had made quick work of the guards they'd run into at the range complex, but he'd still been pissed at how long it had taken to find the weapons and get to the villa. Once outside the wall, they'd spent minimal time planning the rescue. Logan, Holden, Wes, and Trent would come up from the beach and create a distraction, drawing as many of the guards in that direction as they could, while he and Dalton slipped into the house and rescued Bristol.

That plan would have to change a little now that she was already outside, but if the distraction Logan and the others provided was good enough, the original plan could still work.

Then the truck full of ammunition exploded, and Nash thought his heart was going to explode right along with it as he lost sight of the woman he loved behind a fireball nearly as big as the house.

Loved? Hell, yes, he loved her!

Nash was running toward the villa before the debris even hit the ground, terrified that he was already too late and furious at Logan for doing something as stupid as shooting a rocket propelled grenade at a truck load of ammo.

He'd wanted a good distraction, not a friggin' nuclear blast!

As he moved around to the side of the torn apart truck, he realized the explosion had been even worse than he'd feared. The whole side of the villa was on fire. Worse, he couldn't see Bristol anywhere.

"There she is!" Dalton shouted, motioning toward the front of the house as he took down two of Munoz's men. "She's heading back inside."

"Why the hell would she do that?" Nash muttered.

Dalton didn't bother to answer the question, too busy focusing on the group of bad guys heading their way.

Nash raced across the lawn, desperate to catch up to Bristol. Automatic weapon fire from the direction of the beach chewed up the driveway, sending Munoz's men diving for cover and giving Nash and Dalton time to make it to the house.

"Keep going after Bristol," Dalton said, stopping in the doorway and shooting the AK-74 assault back outside. "I'll keep everyone off your tail."

Nash gave him a nod, hoping Dalton knew how much he appreciated what he was doing, then he took off. What the hell was so important that Bristol would run back into a burning building? Had she left something in her bedroom?

He took the steps two at a time, heavy smoke rolling across the ceiling above him. Nash only prayed he was able to find Bristol before it got worse. Another big explosion nearly knocked him off his feet as the whole building shook. Fire roared as it rushed into the villa.

Things had just gotten worse.

Nash reached the top of the stairs when the lights went out. He cursed but kept moving, calling Bristol's name as he checked each room he got to. He almost shot the first maid that hurried out of one of them, coughing and running for the stairs. He got the woman headed in the right direction, warning her in Spanish to go out the back door.

"Bristol, where are you?" he shouted as he reached the end of the long corridor full of rooms without finding her.

She wasn't up there.

He ran back the way he'd come, calling her name over and over. He'd almost gotten to the landing when two of Munoz's men charged up the steps.

Nash didn't stop to shoot, Instead, he tackled the two men, sending all three of them tumbling down the stairs. He lost his rifle at some point during the trip, but couldn't afford to spend time worrying about it.

The moment they came to a stop at the base of the stairs, he slammed his forehead into one man's face, then quickly ripped the second guy's weapon away. Rolling off the pile of arms and legs, he spun around to shoot both men in rapid succession.

Tossing the empty weapon on the floor, Nash scrambled around until he found his rifle. Shouting Bristol's name, he sprinted toward the kitchen. Another explosive fireball tore through the walls and ceiling, bringing intense heat and thick smoke with it.

Shit. This was bad. If he didn't find Bristol soon, it was going to be too late for both of them. Because Nash sure as hell wasn't leaving without her.

He was nearly to the back of the house when he heard coughing. There was no way in hell to identify a person by a cough, but his gut told him it was Bristol.

"Bristol!" he shouted. "Is that you?"

There was more coughing. "Yes. I'm back here. I need help!"

Nash didn't think his heart could beat any faster, but hearing her voice, and knowing that she needed help, had his pulse racing out of control as he sprinted down the smoke-filled hallway.

He found Bristol in one of the servant's bedrooms. Relief coursed through him at the sight of her. She was alive. The urge to run to her, pull her into his arms, and never let her go was overwhelming, but there wasn't time for that. Bristol was kneeling on the floor beside a barely conscious Isabella.

The woman's face was bruised, and she had one arm wrapped around her ribs. Someone had beaten the older woman pretty good. Nash didn't have to work too hard to figure out who. Leon was an asshole who deserved a bullet in the testicles, followed by one in the chest.

"Nash! Thank God," Bristol said when she saw him.

"How bad is Isabella hurt?" Nash asked, dropping to a knee beside her.

Breathing was a little easier on the floor where the smoke wasn't as thick, which was probably the only reason Bristol and Isabella were still alive.

"I think her ribs are broken," Bristol said. "I tried to help her, but once the smoke got to her and she started coughing, she couldn't walk."

Nash moved closer to Isabella. "I can carry you, but it's going to hurt like hell. Are you okay with that?"

He winced as the older woman succumbed to another bout of coughing that left her crying in pain. Even so, she still looked up at him with grateful eyes and nodded.

Nash held his rifle out to Bristol. "Have you ever handled a weapon like this?"

He hated the idea of giving up his weapon, but he couldn't carry Isabella and defend them at the same time.

Bristol shook her head as she reluctantly took it from him. "No. Never."

"The weapon is already loaded and ready to fire. If you see something bad about to happen, don't think. Just point and pull the trigger."

"I'm not sure I can do that."

"You will if you have to."

Gently slipping his arms under Isabella, he scooped her up and got to his feet, then nodded at Bristol. "Let's go. And stay close."

Bristol didn't feel very confident about handling a weapon, but she nodded and stepped closer to Nash, ready to follow him anywhere. Against all odds, the man she loved had found her and she was never going to let anything get between them again.

As she moved with him through the twisting

and turning corridors toward the front of the villa, she considered what she'd just said to herself. She loved Nash.

Loved.

Not liked him a lot.

Not merely cared about him.

Not really appreciated the fact that he'd risked his life for her over and over.

She loved him deep down inside and in a way she could have never even described until now. It was like she'd suddenly discovered her definition of the word had been horribly incomplete and childishly simple until now. Until she'd met Nash and experienced the real thing.

Bristol wanted to throw her arms around him and kiss him until they were both breathless, but now wasn't the time. There were flames and smoke everywhere, and they couldn't take more than a few steps without coughing. The roar of the fire was so loud she couldn't even hear the shooting outside. Maybe that meant the fighting had stopped. She hoped.

They were hurrying through the kitchen when a blur of movement caught her eye. She turned her head to see Leon charging at them with a look of pure rage on his face. She tried to get the rifle up and pointed in the right direction, but it was too late.

Nash must have sensed Leon coming because he turned his shoulder to protect Isabella before the big jackass smashed into him, knocking all three of them to the floor.

Bristol hit the tile hard, sliding across it and slamming into the marble-topped island. The impact knocked the rifle out of her hands and sent pots, knives, and canisters full of kitchen implements everywhere.

Somewhere nearby, Isabella cried out in pain as she bounced onto the floor.

Bristol's first instinct was to run to her, but one look at Nash and Leon and she changed her mind.

Leon had come down on top of Nash and already had that damn knife he always carried aimed right at the center of Nash's chest. Leon shoved with all his weight and it seemed to be taking every ounce of strength for Nash to keep the tip of the blade away from him.

Bristol scrambled around on the floor for the rifle. She was scared to shoot the thing, but Nash had been right. She could do it if she had to.

Her hand found the weapon just as someone

grabbed her from behind, yanking her away from it. She looked over her shoulder to see Chapman. She fought against his hold, jabbing her elbows into him and kicking with her heels. He merely laughed, knowing he was way too strong for her to do any damage.

She screamed in frustration, ramming her elbow into his side again, only to freeze when her father walked into the kitchen, a pistol in his hand. Her gaze darted to Nash. While she'd been dealing with Chapman, Nash had gotten the tip of the knife pointed away from his chest and was now viciously kneeing Leon in the ribs. There was no way he'd be able to deal with both Leon and her father.

Terrified for him, Bristol struggled harder, twisting around in Chapman's grip and punching him in the face as hard as she could. Chapman cursed and slapped her, then grabbed a handful of her hair, holding her still.

"You're going to need to learn how to be nice to me if you want me to keep your father from killing you," he warned.

Out of the corner of her eye, she saw her father aim his weapon at Nash. Nearly drowning in fear, she shoved against Chapman's chest with all her might. It wasn't enough to push him away, but it gave her more than enough space to lift her knee and slam it into his groin.

His face twisting in pain, he took his hand out of her hair, but only so he could wrap his fingers around her throat and squeeze.

Bristol started to choke as her air was cut off. She punched and kicked at him, but her efforts didn't do any good. Chapman was going to kill her.

But even as everything around her began to go dark, she realized she wasn't scared for herself. All she could think about was Nash and what was going to happen to him

A blur of movement off to the right caught her eye and she stared in disbelief as Isabella plunged a big kitchen knife into Chapman's shoulder. He cried out in pain, immediately releasing Bristol. Twisting around to pull the blade out, he strode toward Isabella.

Bristol kneeled on the floor, gulping in air and wanting nothing more than to stay right where she was until she could breathe again. But there wasn't time for that.

Scrambling to her feet, she reached for the rifle she'd dropped earlier, but the two silver briefcases on the floor were closer. She grabbed one of them and swung it at Chapman as hard as she could. The edge of the metal case caught him on the side of the head and he dropped to the floor, unconscious. Or dead. She didn't care which.

Bristol let the case tumble from her numb fingers, grabbing the rifle off the floor. She quickly found the trigger. When she looked up again, what she saw almost stopped her heart.

Nash and Leon were on their knees, still fighting for control of the knife. Her father was a few feet away, his pistol pointed at Nash's head.

If you see something bad about to happen, don't think. Just point and pull the trigger.

After saying a quick prayer, that's what she did.

The weapon bucked multiple times in her hands, the recoil and noise so much worse than she'd expected that she almost dropped it. She wrapped her finger around the trigger again, ready to shoot when her father turned to look at her, shock on his face. He slowly dropped to his knees, the pistol falling from his hand as his eyes rolled up into his head and he tumbled forward.

The distraction was all Nash needed. With

a rapid twist of his hands, he yanked the knife away from Leon and drove the blade deep into his chest, then twisted it. Leon looked stunned someone had finally stabbed him with his own weapon.

Then Nash was up and running toward her. "We have to get out of here before we get trapped by the fire."

Bristol hadn't realized how bad the heat and smoke had gotten until then. It was so hot in the kitchen it felt like they were in an oven. She turned to Isabella, expecting to see Chapman lying on the floor where she'd left him, but he'd disappeared. So had the two briefcases.

Nash quickly picked Isabella up in his arms. "Let's go."

The journey through the fiery house seemed to take forever, and by the time they ran out the front door and moved across the driveway and onto the lawn, Bristol's throat was raw and burning.

The outside of the villa looked as horrible as the inside. There were burning trucks and bullet-riddled cars everywhere. Along with a lot of dead bodies. Her father's men.

She jerked her head up at the sound of gunshots, and she feared for a second that they'd run from near certain death to another situation just as deadly. But then she realized it was only Dalton and another man with dark blond hair and blue eyes. She didn't know him, but Dalton did. They were both shooting at a sedan squealing out of the main gate.

"Who was that?" Nash asked, carefully setting Isabella on the ground and checking her ribs.

"I thought it was you at first," the guy with Dalton said with a grin.

Nash scowled. "I don't look that much like that asshole, Trent."

Trent shrugged. "The guy could be your twin. Besides, at first, I didn't even see his face. Just a guy running out carrying two briefcases, blood running down the side of his head. When we figured out it wasn't you, he made a run for it and ended up dropping one of the briefcases getting away."

Bristol cursed silently. She hated that Chapman had gotten away.

She was still standing there watching the house she'd grown up in smolder and slowly crumble to the ground when Nash came over. "We'll need to get Isabella to a hospital, but she's going to be okay."

She nodded. That was one good thing at least.

Nash wrapped his arms around her. "I'm sorry you had to shoot your father."

"I'm not," she said. "It's something I had to do. For my mother. And for you."

All that might have been true, but it didn't stop the tears from coming. Nash held her close, letting her get it all out.

She wasn't sure how much time passed before he gently lifted her chin. "I have no idea how long the local cops will wait before showing up out here, but we need to go before they do."

Bristol looked one more time at the ruins of the house, then intertwined her fingers with his, her lips curving into a smile. "Let's go home."

CHAPTER
Fourteen

Y OU DON'T HAVE TO BE NERVOUS. WE'RE JUST A GROUP of friends hanging out." Nash flashed her a charming grin as he gave her hand a squeeze. "You'll fit right in. I promise."

Bristol scanned the grassy expanse of San Diego's Waterfront Park, past the interactive water fountains and playgrounds to one of the picnic areas, her hand tightening on the colorfully-wrapped doll they'd brought for the birthday girl. There were at least thirty people gathered around the tables, laughing and having a good time.

She glanced at Nash, surprised at how a single smile from him was enough to make her pulse beat faster. But while she appreciated the gesture and his heartfelt words, she wasn't so sure if she believed him. She didn't know if she was ready to handle a big crowd and the questions that would almost certainly come with it.

She and Nash had only been in San Diego a few days, during which they'd stuck close to his apartment so she could have time to adjust to everything that had happened. She thought she'd been handling it all fairly well, but after they'd gotten to his place and she'd slowed down enough to finally think, everything kind of hit her at once. She cried more tears than she'd shed since her mother had gone missing.

Nash had been incredible. He'd simply held her close and let her cry it out. Then again, he'd been amazing all along. Whether it was getting her a new American passport, buying her a ticket on a plane bound for San Diego, talking to her family in Connecticut, even arranging to have her mother's body found and transported to the States, he'd done it all for her. She couldn't have dealt with any of that stuff on her own.

But more than that, he'd been the rock she leaned on when everything around her was going insane. It was impossible to explain how important that was and how much she loved him for being there for her. So, when he'd suggested she needed to venture out of the apartment and get some sunshine, she'd agreed, even though she hadn't wanted to. After all he'd done for her, she could put up with a little social anxiety.

As she and Nash neared the group of people, Dalton walked over to meet them.

"Hey, you," Dalton said, giving her a hug. "It's good to finally see you out and about. You had us all a little worried."

She smiled. Nash's brash friend had grown on her a lot over the past week. "I'll admit, I wasn't ready, but Nash insisted. He said it would be good for me and he hasn't been wrong yet."

Dalton chuckled. "Who would have thought a guy as dim as he is could say something intelligent every once in a while?"

Bristol couldn't help but laugh. She didn't think she'd ever get used to how these SEALs teased each other all the time. She didn't have brothers and sisters, but if she had, she liked to think it would be like this.

"How's everything back in Manzanillo?" Dalton asked. "Is Isabella doing okay?"

"She's doing fine," Bristol said. "Alejandro is taking good care of her. I think there's a chance they'll finally get married, but only if she agrees to run off on *Lydia's Dream* with him."

They were still laughing about that when Shaw slowly made his way over to them. Nash and Dalton made room so the CIA agent could give her a careful hug. The move was a little awkward, especially with one of his arms in a sling. But that was okay with Bristol. She was glad he was up and walking around. He'd done more than his fair share helping her get out of Mexico along with Nash. She appreciated that. It seemed the CIA appreciated him, too. They'd given him a promotion and a transfer to San Diego.

"You look better than the last time I saw you," Nash pointed out, shaking Shaw's good hand. "Have you started therapy yet?"

Shaw shook his head. "Not yet. Maybe another week or so. Then the real work will start."

"Speaking of work," Dalton said. "Did you ever figure out what happened to Chapman or that Russian arms dealer who sold Munoz those weapons to begin with?"

"No." Shaw frowned. "Both Chapman and Edein Gojkic have completely disappeared off the radar. I imagine they'll turn up soon enough. People like them always do. In fact, one of my responsibilities at my new job is figuring out where the hell they went and what they'll do next. I'm praying we don't see more of those surface-to-air missiles showing up on the black market. That's enough to make me lose sleep at night."

Nash scowled. They'd talked a lot about how weird it was that there was someone out who looked like him going around making the world a crappy place. She hated thinking about it, but she had no doubt that if he was ever given a chance, Nash would go after Chapman simply because of what the man had done to her in the kitchen back at the villa.

"There's something I need to talk to you guys about," Shaw said. "You're not going to like it, but I need you to go along with me on this."

"What is it?" Nash asked.

Shaw took a deep breath. "Neither the CIA nor ATF want it coming out that their agents went rogue. It would be a public relations nightmare. They've slapped a classified coversheet on the whole mess and buried it. The official company line is that both Roman and Santiago were killed in the line of duty trying to take down Munoz. I know it sucks, but I'm asking you to simply keep the details of their part of the mission to yourselves."

Nash and Dalton didn't seem upset, so she

nodded, too.

"On the bright side," Shaw added. "You might be interested in knowing the CIA was really impressed with your work down in Mexico, Nash. They've asked me to extend a job offer to you. They can get you out of the SEALs the moment you say the word."

Bristol's stomach clenched. She wasn't thrilled with the work Nash did for the Navy, but at least when he went on a mission, he was surrounded by people who had his back and protected him like family. She got the feeling the CIA wasn't like that.

Nash chuckled. "Thanks, but no thanks. I've figured out that sneaky covert operations aren't for me. Manzanillo was the first—and last—undercover work this Navy SEAL is ever going to be involved in."

Bristol sagged with relief. That was one less thing to worry about, at least.

"If you change your mind, you know where to find me," Shaw said. "Okay, I'm going to get out of here. Have fun."

As Shaw made his way across the park, a woman with long, blond hair over by the picnic tables called Dalton's name.

"Who's that?" Nash asked.

"That's Beth. She's one of those women I met while we were overseas." Dalton flashed her a smile, then glanced at Nash. "I told you about that, remember?"

Nash nodded.

"Okay, what was that all about?" Bristol asked as Dalton jogged over to Beth. "I thought you said you guys were deployed right before coming to Manzanillo? How did he end up meeting a girl?"

"Yeah, well, apparently a Tinder account can be accessed from anywhere."

"Ah," she said.

Nash smiled. "Come on."

Giving her hand a squeeze, he led her over to the picnic tables where most of the adults were gathered around a cute, little girl with an absolutely angelic face topped with a wild tangle of pale blond hair. She was kneeling on the bench seat, eagerly surveying the stack of gift-wrapped presents in front of her, a huge smile on her face.

Nash introduced Bristol to everyone, making a joke about there being a test later on all the names. She laughed. No way could she remember all of them yet. But she definitely latched onto a few of them, including Kurt Travers, the guy who'd just retired from the SEALs and now worked on Coronado as a civilian. His wife, Melissa, was easy to remember, too.

Lastly, Nash brought her over to see the birthday girl and her parents. She'd met Trent down in Manzanillo, of course, but it was nice finally meeting his wife, Lyla. And their eight-year-old adopted daughter was an absolute darling! Nash had told her that Erika had grown up in a tough situation and that this was her first real birthday, which was why everyone was going a little overboard on the presents. That seemed like an awesome idea to Bristol.

"Hey, Erika. You have room for any more presents?" Nash asked, holding up the wrapped gift and giving the little girl a smile. "Or should I take it back to the store?"

The girl giggled. "There's always room for more presents. Put it right here on top of the stack. I'll open yours first since you're one of my favorite uncles."

Bristol laughed as Nash did exactly as he was told, placing the doll they'd picked out and wrapped together that morning in front of the birthday girl.

"Erika, this is Bristol," Nash said. "She helped

picking out the present, so if you don't like what we got for you, it's all her fault."

Erika giggled again, giving Bristol a wave. "I like your name. It's cool. And I know I'm going to like your present. I love dolls."

Bristol gave Nash a questioning look, wondering if he'd told Erika what they bought, but he seemed as confused as she was.

"What makes you think it's a doll?" Bristol asked.

Erika considered that, pursing her lips and regarding the two of them with a knowing expression that seemed completely out of place on a girl her age. "Well, I know it can be hard for some guys to know what to buy a girl, so before Uncle Nash went off on his trip, I specifically told him that I liked Monster High stuff. Then there's the unique shape of the box, which tells me it's a Monster High doll." Erika gave them a megawatt smile. "Am I right?"

"Maybe you should open it and find out," Nash said.

Erika shook her head. "Nah, I'll wait until after we eat. Mom always says things are better when you have to wait for them a little bit. Right, Mom?"

"That's exactly right," Lyla said, a glimmer of tears in her eyes as Erika jumped up to join the other kids on playground.

"That girl is going to be a heartbreaker," Nash said.

Bristol silently agreed.

A few minutes later, Erika asked Nash and her other uncles—aka SEAL Team 5—to play with her and the other kids.

"You okay here by yourself?" Nash whispered to Bristol.

She laughed. "I'm fine. Go have fun with the kids."

Giving her a quick kiss on the lips, Nash jogged to catch up with his teammates, leaving Bristol sitting with Melissa, Lyla, Hayley Garner, and Felicia Bradford while the guys ran around the park playing some convoluted game of tag.

"Which ones are the kids again?" Felicia asked with a laugh.

Bristol sipped her iced tea. "So, how did you end up meeting your significant others?"

"I met Kurt over twenty-five years ago when he came into my elementary school classroom for career day and balanced a ball on his nose like a seal," Melissa said with a smile. "But I didn't realize the kind of man I was getting involved with until he saved me from three men trying to carjack us on our first date. My heart pretty much belonged to him after that."

Bristol was still staring wide-eyed at Melissa when Hayley laughed. "Chasen saved me from a group of terrorist in Nigeria. And then again right here in San Diego when an old friend had an emotional breakdown and wanted to kill me."

"You're making that up, right?" Bristol asked.

Hayley shook her head. "I'm a journalist and I still can't make stuff up that good. It all happened and Chasen got me through it. I wouldn't be here today without him. But more importantly, I wouldn't know what it means to love someone with my entire soul if it wasn't for him."

Bristol looked at Felicia. "Please tell me you met Logan in the produce section of the grocery store."

Felicia smiled, but shook her head. "Sorry, but nope. I kidnapped Logan at gunpoint because a group of Russian mercenaries were holding my sister hostage. It didn't stop him from rescuing my sister and me. So yeah, I kind of fell in love with a man in shiny armor who goes around saving the world."

"If it makes you feel any better," Lyla said. "I used to crush on Trent all the way back in high school. But our relationship didn't really take off until he and some of his teammates came down to Mexico to rescue Erika and me from drug dealers. Then he agreed to adopt Erika with me because he knew she needed a family. So, Trent's my hero, too."

Bristol shook her head. "And here I thought Nash was the only one who's a superhero."

"Of course, he's a superhero," Melissa said. "They're SEALs. It's what they do."

Felicia nibbled on a tortilla chip. "So, how did you and Nash meet?"

Bristol only meant to give them the CliffsNotes version like they'd done, but she ended up telling them everything. Maybe because the women could understand exactly what she'd been through. By the time she was finished, there wasn't a dry eye at the table.

"It sounds crazy after everything that happened, but sometimes I can't help wondering how I got so lucky Nash showed up," she said. "I don't want to imagine what would have happened if he hadn't come into my life when he did."

Hayley reached across the table to give her

hand a squeeze. "Well, you don't need to worry about that. He's in your life now and I'm pretty sure he's not going anywhere."

Bristol wished she could be so sure. She wanted to stay in San Diego and make a life with Nash, but she didn't know what he wanted. Things happened down in Manzanillo so fast. What if he regretted his decision to bring her back with him?

"Have you thought about what kind of work you'd like to do here in San Diego?" Felicia asked. "Nash said you have a background in tourism and travel."

Bristol nodded, admitting how it had been her dream to open her own business and specialize in vacation packages to exotic locales.

"Would you be willing to work for someone else if it meant getting to do that dream job?" Felicia asked.

Bristol wasn't sure where this was going. "Yeah, I guess so."

"I'm a wedding planner, but I want to branch out and start offering honeymoon packages," Felicia explained. "What do you think of putting together exotic honeymoon adventures?"

Bristol smiled, already thinking of the possibilities. "I think that sounds fantastic. I'm in!"

She and Felicia were exchanging phone numbers when the game of tag ended and Nash jogged over with Erika and the guys, laughing and ready to eat. Sitting down beside Bristol, he gave her a kiss that made her wonder why she even doubted how he felt about her. That said, she'd feel a whole lot better if she knew for sure.

⚓

"You were quiet on the way home," Nash said as they walked into his apartment.

Bristol smiled as they collapsed on the couch. The place was a one-bedroom with a small kitchen and a mid-sized living room. There wasn't even room for a coat closet. The whole apartment could have fit in the garage at the villa. Or at least in the garage that had been there before the villa was destroyed. Regardless of how big it was or wasn't, she loved this apartment. Because this is where Nash was.

"I'm just a little tired," she said, leaning against him.

He wrapped an arm around her, caressing her bare skin with the tips of his fingers. "We didn't have to stay so late if you didn't want to."

"I know, but I was having a good time," she said. "Felicia, Melissa, and all the other women are so amazing. I just met them and yet it's already starting to feel like I have a new family."

"But?" When she didn't answer, he shifted on the couch so he could look at her. "There's obviously something you want to talk about, so out with it."

She sighed. "I was talking to Felicia and the other women about what happened down in Mexico, how we met, and how you saved my life. I told them how I felt lucky to have you in my life."

He grinned. "I feel pretty lucky myself."

"Really?"

"Yeah." He frowned. "What's wrong? Are you having second thoughts about staying here with me?"

"No! Of course not!"

He looked even more confused. "But?"

Bristol hesitated. She'd lost everything in the world she'd known, and she didn't want to lose Nash, too.

"I'm in love with you, Nash." The words came out in a rush and she hurried on before he could say anything. "When we were in Manzanillo, you said you wanted me to come home to San Diego with you, but now that I'm here, it feels like someone has hit the pause button. I'm trying hard not to read too much into it, but I can't help it. I'm starting to freak out a little because I don't know how you feel about me."

She held her breath, on the verge of tears for some ridiculous reason. *Crap.* What if she'd just ruined everything?

Bristol waited for Nash to say something. Anything. But what she got was a chuckle.

Inexplicable anger shot through her and she pulled her hands away from his. She'd poured her heart out to him and he was *laughing*? "What's so funny?"

"Nothing." He stopped laughing, but he couldn't seem to wipe the smile completely off his face. "I'm relieved, that's all."

Now it was her turn to be confused. "Relieved?"

He reached up to brush her hair back. "I thought you were trying to find a way to tell me you were dumping me."

Her mouth may have dropped open. She wasn't paying enough attention to her own body to know for sure. She was too focused on Nash's unbelievable confession. He'd been worried *she* was dumping *him*?

She started to ask him what made him think such a crazy thing, but Nash placed a gentle finger on her lips. "I love you, Bristol. I think I have from the moment I saw you on the steps of the villa. I probably should have told you sooner, but I assumed you'd know how much I care about you since I was willing to die to keep you safe. Now I know that's not enough. So, I promise to tell you every day what you mean to me."

Bristol tried to reply, but he shook his head, his finger still on her lips. "I want you to stay here with me. It's what I wanted when I asked you to come to San Diego. I thought that was obvious already, but if it isn't, I'll make it official."

Taking his finger away from her lips, he leaned forward and kissed her with all the feeling in the world. Her heart beat harder as his fingers slipped into her hair and held her firmly, his tongue teasing hers until she was dizzy. Only then did he pull back. But he kept his fingers wrapped up in her hair.

"Bristol Munoz, I want you in my life, in my apartment, and in my bed. But more than that, I want you as my wife to have and hold until the end of our days."

She blinked, her heart doing a flip followed by what she was sure was a barrel roll. "Is that a proposal?"

"No, that's a promise." He grinned. "The proposal will come later when there's zero doubt in your heart that I'm the man you're going to love forever, and who will love you the same way in return. Trust me, when I ask you to marry me, you'll know it because it'll sweep you off your feet."

Part of her wanted to scream in frustration. If Nash had asked her to marry him right then, she would have said yes on the spot. She could live with a promise, though. But only because she believed him when he said he loved her. The relief that washed over her was hard to describe. It was like she could finally breathe again.

She leaned forward and kissed him as gently as he'd kissed her, and with as much conviction. "Thank you."

"For what?" he asked, the corner of his mouth tipping up.

"For showing up in my life, putting yourself at risk, saving me, and bringing me here to San Diego with you. But mostly, for loving me. I guess that's what I needed more than anything else. For you to simply love me."

He chuckled. "If loving is what you need, why don't I take you to our bed so I can spend the rest of the night showing you exactly how much I do love you. Just without so many words."

"Our bed." Bristol smiled and kissed him again. "I like the sound of that."

I hope you enjoyed Nash and Bristol's story!
Want more hunky SEALs?

Check out the other books in the *SEALs of Coronado Series*!
SEAL for Her Protection
Strong Silent SEAL
Texas SEAL
SEAL with a Past
SEAL to the Rescue

paigetylertheauthor.com/books/#coronado

Sign up for Paige Tyler's New Releases mailing list and get a FREE copy of SEAL of HER DREAMS!

Visit
www.paigetylertheauthor.com

For more Military Heroes check out my X-OPS
and SWAT Series!

X-OPS

Her Perfect Mate

Her Lone Wolf

Her Wild Hero

Her Fierce Warrior

Her Rogue Alpha

Her True Match

Her Dark Half

Exposed

paigetylertheauthor.com/books/#ops

SWAT (SPECIAL WOLF ALPHA TEAM)

Hungry Like the Wolf

Wolf Trouble

In the Company of Wolves

To Love a Wolf

Wolf Unleashed

Wolf Hunt

Wolf Hunger

Wolf Rising

paigetylertheauthor.com/books/#wolf

ABOUT PAIGE

Paige Tyler is a *New York Times* and *USA Today* Bestselling Author of sexy, romantic suspense and paranormal romance. She and her very own military hero (also known as her husband) live on the beautiful Florida coast with their adorable fur baby (also known as their dog). Paige graduated with a degree in education, but decided to pursue her passion and write books about hunky alpha males and the kick-butt heroines who fall in love with them.

www.paigetylertheauthor.com

CPSIA information can be obtained
at www.ICGtesting.com
Printed in the USA
BVHW070815240521
607995BV00004B/125